Puffin Books Editor: Kaye Webb

D1146993

COME HOME, BRUMBY

Mary Elwyn Patchett

'Any news, son?' called Jim Meehan, but Joey simply shook his head. It was weeks now since Brumby, the wild stallion, had led his herd away on their seasonal migration, and Florian, the beautiful white stallion whom Joey had tamed, had escaped from his paddock to follow them.

There wasn't much hope of news now, for the herd had disappeared in the direction of the Snowy Mountains, where they might succumb to the bitter weather, or they might have been shot by brumby hunters on the way. But Joey couldn't let it rest at that. For years now he had dreamed of fencing in the brumby herd and breeding to improve the stock, and so he decided to follow the herd himself.

Though he was still only fifteen and the brumbies' tracks had long since disappeared, he was determined to find them somehow, and to drive them home single-handed.

It was a heroic undertaking, one that most boys would never have even considered, but Joey had the courage of a grown man, and possibly, with his knowledge of the bush, he might even succeed.

For readers of nine and over.

Cover design by David Carl Forbes.

He took her across in a beautiful clean jump

Mary Elwyn Patchett

Come Home, Brumby

Illustrated by
Stuart Tresilian

Penguin Books

Penguin Books Ltd, Harmondsworth,
Middlesex, England
Penguin Books Australia Ltd, Ringwood,
Victoria, Australia

First published by Lutterworth Press 1961
Published in Puffin Books 1972
Copyright © Mary Elwyn Patchett, 1961

Made and printed in Great Britain by
Richard Clay (The Chaucer Press) Ltd,
Bungay, Suffolk
Set in Linotype Pilgrim

Part One

Jim Meehan stepped out of the stable door with a worried frown on his brown face. The stall was empty. It should have held Moonlight, the beautiful little white mare whose head had once been hideously mutilated on one side by a brutal captor before Jim, and his son Joey, had rescued her.

Moonlight ran freely with the brumby herd, the band of wild horses that made their headquarters on the red, rocky hill that towered beyond the Meehans' little shack. When the fancy took them this herd thundered down the hill, across the river flats and away for one month, perhaps two; but in the seven years of their occupation they had never stayed away longer than that, until this year.

Sometimes Moonlight went off with the herd, and although Joey worried about her, as indeed he did about the rest of the herd, both father and son believed that to run with the herd was a part of her natural joy in living, and they never tried to stop her. Joey always knew that one day she would return, that one day he would go into her loose-box and see that his small white unicorn was back again, and she would be as exquisitely aloof as ever.

It was a one-sided love-affair between Joey and Moonlight. He felt humbly grateful that she trusted him and was even known to turn to him in times of trouble, but she never showed him affection; her first meeting with man had been too terrible to be forgotten, and her animal brain could not reason that after the first brutality, the things which Jim and Joey had to do, the often painful efforts to restore her to normality, were not just a continuance of man's cruelty and power.

Moonlight's first son by Brumby was called Florian. Brumby was the core of Joey's heart. He had been born when Joey was a little fellow, barely eight years old. Brumby had gone, of course – he was the leader of the herd, a wild silver stallion of great power and intelligence, and it was understandable that Moonlight had gone with him. But why had Florian gone too? This Joey could not understand, nor could Jim, and he mourned for Joey's unhappiness. Also, being a practical bushman, he was upset at the thought of losing more of the stud-fees which Florian had been earning in the past year or two.

It was true that Florian was of brumby stock, but no man, least of all a bushman, could look at the stallion and doubt that here was a thoroughbred. There were no blood-lines in the stud book to proclaim Florian a champion, but he became talked about beyond the little township of Conway's Flat. The owners of personable mares were only too glad to get such a fine strain among their stock, although the stud-fee, which helped the Meehans so much, was not an eighth of what it would have been if Florian had been of provable blood-stock.

Jim, leaning against the stable wall, heard the sound of hooves and his face lit up. He thought that Joey was coming home. He was wrong. It was his neighbour, Geoff Brett, coming towards him.

'Hi, Jim! Any news of Florian and the brumbies?'

Jim shook his head. 'Joey's not home yet, I dunno if he's found anything.'

Geoff slouched sideways to ease his tired body in the

saddle and tilted his old felt hat over his eyes as his gnarled fingers scrabbled at the back of his head.

'Thought I'd ask on me way home. I'd better git on. You an' Joey can count on us if you can think of anythin' ter do – see yer tomorrer.' He straightened up in the saddle and urged his weary horse on the last lap for home.

Jim watched him disappear down the hill without his eyes really seeing him. He was thinking of the time when Joey found the little smoky foal standing by his mother, Moonlight, legs spread, tiny hooves firmly on the ground. Florian had been Joey's first foal from the brumby herd he loved so dearly. Together he and his father guided the silvery mare back to her stable and little Florian followed with stumping, baby footsteps, too young to be astonished by a world in which every sound, every trick of light and living were being seen for the first time. He followed his mother into her dry, comfortable stable.

During Florian's babyhood, as long as his mother fed him, they lived in the stable and exercised in the paddock on the far side of the shack, which was the only piece of their property that Joey and his father had been able to fence in. It was a sizeable piece of land, taking in the grassy sweep of a low hill, and a good watering place with a small sandy beach on the little creek meandering its way between Geoff and Rowena Brett's property, Euro Downs, and Jim's unnamed land. From there the fence climbed the hill again, across the stony ground so necessary for healthy hooves in wild or domesticated horses, and embraced a shady belt of bushland spicy with eucalypts, sturdy iron barks and the yellow box that the wild bees love.

Jim Meehan leaned against the empty stable door and pondered again what would make a tamed, affectionate

stallion, living in contentment for years, knock a rail out
of the fence and follow a wild herd. At least, they could
only suppose that Florian had gone after the wild horses,
perhaps incited by Moonlight from outside the fence.
There had been the marks of Florian's hooves where he
had pushed and kicked at the loose top rail and jumped
the lower one. Then the double trail, the elegant small-
ness of Moonlight's tracks, the big deep pits of Florian's.

It had not been loneliness, for Florian always had
several mares in his paddock. Trixie, the old half-draft
mare, had been turned out to grass there after a lifetime
of service. When Florian was a yearling Joey's horse,
Flash, had been there. Flash was a poor ancient beast
given him by Geoff Brett and greatly treasured by the
boy. But Flash, surrounded by loving care, lay down one
evening and never rose again. Even Joey could not
greatly mourn his peaceful death.

Now there was usually some youngster of Florian's
sireing playing in the paddock, and Jim's three cows and
their calves made added company. No, it was not loneliness that drove Florian to join Brumby's herd, or perhaps
just to follow it. Apart from Joey's anxiety, Florian was
a monetary loss the Meehans would find it hard to survive.

Brumby, Florian's sire, was the sagacious leader of a
herd of fine animals and he would brook no challenge
from any other stallion. Sometimes Jim and Joey captured yearlings from Brumby's herd and sold them as
geldings. The male youngsters left in the herd were dealt
with by Brumby not much later than in their second
year; his savage teeth and flailing hooves sent them
about their business. They would run disconsolately for
a while then, if lucky, pick up a mare or several mares to
form the nucleus of their own herds. More often, being
without the necessary bushcraft, they fell victims to

the brumby shooters that harried the herds every year.

Now Florian, who had been bred up to civilized living, whose natural instincts had been blunted, was missing and the herd had gone. It was no wonder that Joey was worried. Jim sighed. Ever since Joey had been a little bloke of barely seven he had dreamed of fencing in and owning the splendid brumby herd. If that happened, instead of stealing mares as did Brumby, in common with all wild stallions when he was on 'walkabouts' and struggling instinctively against in-breeding, the Meehans would choose his mares, keeping a balance between the youngsters allowed to grow up with the herd and the new stock. This could be done in a way that was not possible when every year the herd swept down the hillside to disappear for months.

Joey always worried when the herd went off, knowing that brumby hunters might attack the mob, but his faith and pride in Brumby as the leader kept the boy from too much apprehension.

Over the years with help and hard work from their neighbours Geoff and Bill Regan, they had at last managed to fence in most of the great hill which, out of a sort of geographical politeness, they called 'the mountain'. Now there was not much more than three miles to fence to complete the job.

For years they searched out and cut down box timber because it was the hardest and best for post-and-rail fencing, and they had no money for any other kind. Besides, wire fencing was too dangerous around wild horses. The three men, the boy and sometimes Rowena, Geoff's wife, dragged and split the posts and rails twelve inches wide, dug the two-feet-deep post holes often in hard, rocky soil, cleared the timber on either side when it might fall and damage their fence, measuring the actual fence in ten-foot panels.

During the current year they all worked feverishly from the day the brumbies swept down the mountain and away, so that before the horses returned Joey's dream might be realized.

'Poor little bloke,' Jim thought, 'so near, so far!' Well, he took it like the man he was, but his friends and his father knew how deeply disappointed and worried he felt.

Jim moved his lounging shoulders from the stable wall and began to roll a cigarette. He glanced down the windswept hillside and his grey eyes lit up. Coming up from the creek he saw the rather ugly brown head of Joey's horse. Joey called this horse Yarraman, which is an Abo word for 'horse', and it was after the present Yarraman's sire who had been leader of the mob before Brumby's day. He had been a big ugly-headed, terrible-tempered brown stallion, coarse and powerful, full of fight and fire, and had been betrayed to his death by the same callous brute who had smashed his gun-butt down on Moonlight's delicate head.

Joey had taken one of Yarraman's foals, and it had grown into a fast, tireless beast with the great heart of the father. Yarraman loved only Joey, who had given him infinite patience and affection. Now, rising eight years, Yarraman was at the top of his power. Joey liked the tireless feel of his mount, and while he recognized that Yarraman had none of the aristocratic pride and delicacy of the Brumby strain, he would not have changed him in any way. He also felt that, as a man, he should repay a little of the debt that man owed Yarraman's treacherously slain sire.

Jim walked to the fence and leaned his arms along the top rail, smoking quietly, as he watched the big brown horse lurching up the hillside carrying his son. He thought of the small Joey, a thin, tow-headed, intense wisp of a child, riding his first horse, old Flash, up the hillside as he returned from his morning postal lessons given him by Rowena Brett. Jim reflected that he could never repay Rowena, the tall, gaunt bushwoman who had once been a schoolteacher, for all that she had done for Joey, and most of all, he could never repay her for the love she gave him.

Joey 'cooeed' to his father. He liked to see Jim there waiting for him when he rode home, especially now when he was so worried over Brumby and his herd.

'Any news, son?' Jim called.

Joey shook his head. At fifteen he was a tall boy with a slim, sinewy body. Eight years with his father had turned him into a hardened, experienced bushman. He had a quick mind and learned easily, passing every exam in the postal lessons Rowena gave him. He was as brown as a burnt almond and his blue eyes were very blue indeed as they looked from the sun-wrinkles of his young face. His hair, although it had darkened a little with the years, still showed tow-coloured streaks burnt into it by the ever-hungry sun.

All his remembered life Joey wanted more than anything else to be the sort of man his father wanted him to be. Next to that wish he had a devouring need to fence their land as a protection for the brumby herd. He had big plans for allowing his herd limited freedom to build champions, guided by the wisdom of man.

This was a dream of which his father and his friends thoroughly approved, but its realization would be an expensive one. None of the men concerned in it had much money. In the past year only sheer toil made the fence lengthen. Joey believed that unless the herd had plenty of room to move about in the whole scheme would flop. What proved to be more than sixteen miles of fencing was on its last lap when the herd began their seasonal migration; this time they had not returned, and Moonlight and Florian were apparently with them.

Jim eyed with pride the loose, balanced movements of his son in the saddle as the big horse pulled himself up the hill. Joey certainly had a way with horses, and with dogs, he added to himself as a big, gaunt wolf-like dog trotted up the hill and slipped into the stable to wait for Joey, its master, and Yarraman, its devoted friend.

'Hang on, I'll take the bar off the gate for yer.' Jim opened the rough wooden gate and Joey rode in and slid off Yarraman's tall back.

'Thanks, Dad. Yarraman always wants to kick it down when he's waiting for his feed.'

Joey grinned at his father, then gave his horse's hairy brown ear an affectionate tug before he undid the girth, pulled off the saddle and lifted it on to the peg in the stable wall. Yarraman turned his ugly, intelligent head and nuzzled the back of Joey's shirt until he wriggled his body and said, 'Hey! Stop that! You tickle!' He rubbed his horse down and turned him out in the back paddock to feed. Then he joined his father, after stooping to pat the big dog with an 'Off you go, Wolf,' knowing that Wolf would stay beside Yarraman all the night.

As the two walked towards the shack, Jim saw Joey turn his head and glance towards the mountain, and knew why. He shook his head.

'No, son, they're not back, but don't give up hope.' They both stopped, and together their eyes searched the great hill where, from the homestead side, they could not see the big hollow amphitheatre edged by red 'organ pipe' rocks that made the secluded enclosure the wild horses loved. The men could not resist gazing at it with eyes that had more of prayer in them than hope of realization. Joey looked up at his father.

'You know I won't give up hoping, not ever, but now I want to *do* something about getting them home.'

The two Meehans went into the shack that was all the home Joey had ever known. No home was ever simpler. It was one long room broken by glassless spaces in the walls that were the windows; the men's bunks were built at either end, the middle of the room was living space and kitchen. At one end a door led out to a small lean-to where Jim had fixed up a shower bath. The floor was of concrete, and the shower an old galvanized iron oil-tin which had holes punched in the bottom. This could be lowered by a pulley to have a bucket of water dumped in it and hauled up again. When a piece of string was pulled the water was released and if you were quick you could do a rapid soaping and then rinse it off. If you were not quick, then you remained soapy, which was only slightly better than having a body caked by the day's sweat.

Jim put his hand on his son's shoulder. 'You git along to the shower, Joey. I'll take a look at what's on the stove.'

Joey went through the back door and Jim turned towards the small wood-burning stove and stirred the rabbit-stew with a long iron spoon.

The room had changed little as Joey grew up. More books and bookshelves had been added. Some of the books had been ordered from town booksellers, others were the residue from the small library in Conway's Flat which Joey had picked up for a few pence, and most of the books were on the care and breeding of horses. The rough grey timber walls were brightened by gay pictures taken from magazines; as they became too fly-spotted Joey and Rowena cut out other pictures to replace them. Now there was a coloured reproduction of the great horse, 'Carbine', and another that made a gay red splash against the grey. It was a double-spread from an English magazine picturing the Life Guards parading through Hyde Park, wearing their glorious uniforms. The beautiful grey horse in the lead, the plumed helmet and red cloak of the officer and the colourful line of men on their darker horses, delighted Joey.

Through the back wall Joey heard the snuffling and impatient whines of his dog, Rebel. He smiled and went out of the shack to let him off the chain.

'Come on boy, keep still while I take your collar off . . . whoah now, give me a look at that foot . . . here, stop it, keep still, there's a good boy.' He put down Reb's injured paw, patted him and let him go to run in wild circles of excitement. Reb was a handsome dog, part dingo, part 'bluey' and goodness knows what else. Joey watched Reb's muscular hindquarters disappearing in the direction of the stable. There had long been a pact of mutual respect between Reb and Wolf and Joey knew that Reb was off to visit Wolf and Yarraman. He would return panting and ecstatic once more, in a way that was out of character for the silent, efficient dog he was.

'Ready for tucker when you are, Dad. I'll just give Reb his, he'll be back in a minute for it.'

Reb usually hunted his own food, but to help the healing of his paw Joey had a rabbit for him. He threw it to the returning Reb who lay down outside the open door, watching Joey as he sat down to his own meal, while Reb tore his dinner to shreds.

Joey and his father ate silently. Jim, usually a silent man, asked no questions. He knew that Joey would talk to him when he was ready; right now he needed food. Jim was a man to whom first things were first. Their plates empty, they sat back, and Jim asked:

'Reb's paw O.K. again?'

'Yes, he's right. Stay there while I clear away, we've got to have a talk.'

Jim rose and stretched. 'Come on, we'll both give it a go an' then we can talk.'

They carried the plates over to the shelf beside the stove and rinsed them as best they could in the small amount of water that could be spared for the job. The nights were cold, the days brilliant and beautiful. In the early morning the brown stubble of the grass was covered in thick white frost, for it was the end of May, and so almost mid-winter. This made the disappearance of the wild herd even more puzzling. The horses usually disappeared when the spring, as it does with every living thing, stirred in their bodies, and the need to roam, to adventure, to make love and to conquer drove them forth.

Joey sat down at one side of the rough, home-made table, and Jim sat at the other and rolled his after-dinner cigarette, while he waited for Joey to tell him what was on his mind.

'Dad,' Joey began, searching for words, 'I've been thinking. I talked to Rowena today, and she thinks I'm on the right track, but she wouldn't say much in case you didn't want to back me up.'

Jim looked at his son with lazy, amused eyes. He knew that however conversation began it would eventually lead to the disappearance of the brumbies. He said,

'When have I ever not "backed you up", son?'

Joey smiled back at him. 'I know – but this is – well, it's different. You may think I'm guessing wrong...'

'Come on, tell me about it.'

'All right. Well, you remember how I went as I always do to see which way Brumby headed the herd the morning after they went off, an' this time it wasn't north-west, the way it's always been before; it was a little south of west. If they went on more or less that way they'd reach the Snowy Mountains, and if they did that then they'd be right there in the real winter weather. I don't think they've been that way before. It worries me, they mightn't know how to live in the cold and the snow. Thank goodness there are no foals with the mob as far as I know, only colts rising yearlings.'

'You may be right, boy, but what d'you think you can do about it?'

'Go after them.'

'"Go after them"! But Joey, you've never been that way yourself, come to think of it, neither 'ave I. Their trail's gone months ago, you can't follow a month-old track. If you went it'd just be guess-work.'

'Geoff knows that country, he'll draw me a map.'

'But . . .'

'Hold on, Dad. There're properties on the way. Some-one's sure to've seen the herd going through; even Brumby isn't clever enough to avoid that.'

'Yes,' Jim thought to himself, although he did not say it aloud to add to Joey's worries, 'and one look at that fine mob an' the brumby runners're as like as not to be out in full force.' Aloud he said.

'D'you want me to go with you?'

Joey's eyes were full of gratitude. 'No, thanks Dad, Reb and I can make it alone. It'll be best that way, and besides, I want you on another job.'

'Wait a minute, boy, supposing you do find Brumby's mob, what're you goin' to do then?'

'Bring them home.'

'What! Drive a wild herd like that one – a mob led by Brumby!' His father's voice was full of disbelief, but Joey answered calmly,

'It's because I know Brumby and his ways so well, and

because, up to a point, he knows me that I believe I can do it.'

'You've forgotten Florian, haven't you? It's a toss-up which of the stallions'll be leading the herd when you catch up with it!'

'I haven't forgotten Florian. I'm hoping they'll both be all right. It could be they've split the herd, such a thing has been known, you told me so yourself; or that Florian's picked-up stray mares on his way and is following the old fellow, but with his own herd.'

Jim looked doubtful. 'It could be, but it's not very likely. Face it, son, the chances are they fought to the death within the first few days. If Florian won because he's young and strong, that still leaves him without the know-how of old Brumby. He won't be as efficient with the herd, nor as good in the bush, and although neither of them knows the mountains or snow conditions, Brumby'll still have the best chance of survival there because he's always had to fend for himself.'

'I know, that makes another reason why I must go. Even if I only bring Florian back it'll be something.'

Jim looked away from the wistful expression in his boy's eyes. He knew better than anyone, except perhaps Rowena, what 'his' herd meant to Joey, he knew what the past months had cost him in enforced inaction. He considered the whole question while Joey sat quietly before him, content to respect his father's advice and his judgement, but ready to fight for his right to do his utmost to protect the herd. Jim decided that it would be intolerable for Joey if he asked him not to go after the herd. It would be better for the boy to try and to fail, as he feared he would do, than to make no move at all and perhaps have that fine herd trapped or shot by men who prowled the land like wolves, waiting to pick up a good horse, or to destroy others who ate grass needed for stock. He nodded his head.

'All right, Joey. When d'you want to start?'

Joey's eyes glowed with pleasure and gratitude.

'As soon as I can get off, but there's one other thing. If I bring the herd back, I'd like to know that the fence is finished to keep them in – I don't want this every year.'

'That's reasonable. But how . . .'

Joey shook his head. 'I know, you're going to say how can it be done? But when you've talked to Geoff and Bill I'm sure you'll see there's a chance. There're about three miles more of tough fencing, the posts're there, and work's not too heavy for any of you at this time. Geoff and Bill, even Rowena say they'll give it a go pretty nearly full time, if you will too. I reckon I ought to be back here with the herd in a month or so. Geoff said to ask you, but he thinks you three could finish the fence in a month, especially with a bit of help from Rowena; she's as good as any man.'

'Hmm, we might do it if it's all straight-ahead work. Joey, don't be too disappointed if you find the mob but can't get them back here. It'll be pretty near impossible to drive them if they don't want to come this way, you know that. Anyway, if you can make it, then we'd better put out brush wings so that they don't go past a fence that'll be new to them, and we'll leave a good gap for them to go through.'

'Yes, a long curved wing'll be best, on the river side of the gap. But Dad, even if I can find them and get Florian, then bring the rest of the herd away from the cold country towards our land, I reckon it'll be worth it.'

Jim looked at his son's earnest face, but he only said quietly,

'I reckon it will, son.'

*

Next day Joey and his father rode over to the homestead at Euro Downs, which was about a mile away across the creek.

After a careful look at Reb's foot, Joey let him follow. It seemed quite sound, and he wanted his dog to harden up before they began the long ride after the herd. Jocy knew that his chances of bringing the herd back were small, but without Reb he would have no chance at all, for even Wolf could not equal Reb as a worker of cattle and horses.

Rowena and Geoff were on the veranda talking to Bill Regan, waiting for Jim and Joey to join them at smoko over cups of tea and hot scones. Rowena was more than ten years older than her husband; she was taller too, with a spare figure and an austere face, her hair in a neat knot on her neck, and she was dressed in a long, old-fashioned skirt and severe blouse. Geoff was an easygoing man who would have been plump if he had not had to work so hard. For Geoff, as for Rowena, Joey was the core of his heart. They had loved him dearly ever since, as a skinny, white-faced wisp of a little boy, he had come back from Sydney with Jim, a child who tried so valiantly never to be less of a man than his father wanted him to be. He put his confiding little paw into Geoff's big palm, and the affection awakened between them had never faltered. Bill Regan was a different type of man from Geoff. He had a hard face and a warm heart, and Joey had the comfortable feeling from the first that whatever he did, whatever happened in his life, Bill was on his side.

It was a tribute to the sweetness of character that was in Joey that these four loving and lonely grown-ups never spoiled him. They gave him all that was in their power to give, but most of all they gave him the love his lonely little heart needed, and he never let them down.

Now, in spite of their age and experience, they listened respectfully to Joey's plans, discussed them with him and offered suggestions, and they did not discourage him. None of them believed he could find and bring back the brumby herd, but out of their respect for him they believed that he should try.

Joey balanced his coffee cup on the arm of the long squatter's chair in which he sat, and smiled across at Rowena, sitting stiffly upright in her old rocking chair.

'Don't worry, I'll be warm,' he assured her. 'I'm going to wear "the bear".'

Rowena smiled back at him. 'I had a feeling that one day it'd come in handy.'

'You didn't think so the day Joey brought that sackful of rabbit-skins over to you and asked you to help him make a jacket!'

'Those smelly old skins! Anyway, now I'm glad that in the end we didn't make too bad a job of tanning and cutting.'

'You christened me "the bear" when I wore the jacket, it was so big for me, so I reckon that now it ought to just about fit me.'

'As it's fur on the outside and lined with an old coat of Geoff's, it ought to be pretty warm. Oh, I've something else for you to take, Joey.'

Rowena rose and went into the house. Geoff grinned.

'You won't freeze if Rowena can help it, Joey!'

'You'll need everything you can take if you 'ave to sleep out in the cold of them mountains,' Bill said.

'I've never seen snow. In a way I hope I have to go pretty high, so long's the herd's all right.'

Rowena returned with two pairs of thick, hand-knitted gloves, and the same in socks.

'I made these for Geoff, but he has plenty. Anyway he

won't wear the gloves, although he grumbles about his hands getting too stiff for milking.'

Joey took the bundle from her. 'Thanks, Rowena, but I won't need two pairs of gloves, will I?'

'Yes you will, and I wish I had another pair of socks for you. If you get wet, you must have a dry pair or you'll be colder than ever.'

'What Joey'll need's a couple of pack-horses before you're finished,' Jim told her, but inwardly he was grateful for Rowena's helpful commonsense. Joey turned to Geoff.

'What about that map, Geoff? That's something I must have.'

Geoff nodded and went indoors, coming back with the stub of a pencil and a big piece of white paper. They pushed back the tea things and Geoff sat at the table while Joey leaned against his shoulder and peered down at the paper. With his bushman's memory for detail of land once seen, of trees and creeks and skylines, Geoff drew Joey the most detailed map he could. When he finished drawing and discussing the various landmarks with Joey, he threw the stub down and turned to the boy.

'Now, the first homestead you stop at, show them this map and see if they can add anything to it.'

Joey nodded, thanked him and folded the paper, putting it in his pocket. He said to Geoff,

'You're all helping, but still I wouldn't have a hope without Reb. It's a good thing his paw's right again.'

Reb, stretched across Joey's feet, opened a sleepy eye when he heard his name. He was a strange-looking dog, medium-sized, powerful, outwardly more like his dingo father than his cattle-dog mother. Old Queenie had been Geoff's dog for years, and she was a wonderful cattle-dog. Then, one night when the moon was high and the sad double-cry of a dingo floated up from the banks of the creek, Queenie, who had never had pups in all her nine years, went off courting with a wild yellow dog. Queenie slowed up somewhat before the birth of her pups, but she still insisted on mustering cattle with Geoff. One day a steer kicked her; before she died she gave birth to a litter of three pups, of which only one was born alive.

Between them Joey and Rowena brought up the pup. Joey and Reb became inseparable. Reb was now four, and he was as fine a cattle-dog as his mother had been. He was a silent worker with the deep silence inherited from his father, the strain of wild blood gave him a strength and single-hearted love for his master to match his silence.

It is this dingo strain that is said to make 'blueys' the finest of all cattle-dogs, heeling cattle low, but Reb, with more than his share of dingo blood, had the stamina and bush sense of what were considered his more disreputable ancestors. Reb was pleasant to all his human friends, but he really loved only Joey, and to a lesser extent Wolf and Yarraman.

Often on moonlit nights Joey would stand in the open door of the shack and watch Reb and Wolf at their wild-dog games with Yarraman, whose own wild strain was in some ways more prepotent than the dogs'. The two dogs stalked the powerful, ugly horse, nipping his heels, swerving as Yarraman kicked out, circling him, sometimes running him in rings until the circle narrowed and the horse stopped with the dogs crouching alertly before him. If Joey could only have one helper, then he was content that it should be Reb.

Jim and Joey rode homewards to get ready for an early start next morning. As Joey rode away the fencers would begin their toil. If they were to finish the job in one month there was not a minute to lose.

Joey was too excited to sleep soundly that night. He slept for a couple of hours, then tossed and turned until he dropped off, and was awake before daylight to light the stove and to get breakfast for them both. Breakfast over, they checked Joey's belongings – the light groundsheet to keep him dry; the soft leather valise packed with warm clothes; the billy attached to his saddle, the saddlebags in which Rowena had packed food for a day or so, and all the other paraphernalia a bushman needs for a month's camping.

Geoff insisted on Joey taking a strong young mare of his to carry his pack. She would double as a second mount and so Joey could travel faster. When he turned the mob on the route home, the mare could be driven with the herd, Joey told himself, and with her homing instinct she would be a steadying influence on the other mares among the wild horses.

Joey expected to cover about forty miles a day, and to slow up on the days when he believed he was drawing near the herd. He would need Yarraman fresh for that. He calculated the minimum distance between his home and the wild horses must be around a hundred and eighty miles. Even with Joey's light weight to carry, the trip would be quite a test of Yarraman's stamina. He hoped to reach the herd in a week to ten days. The return would be slower; the wild horses must be persuaded, they could not be driven. Like his father, he set his jaw and put first things first, and the first thing of all was to find the mob, and Florian.

The morning air was very sharp, the grey shadows of the night still about them and the frost crackling under their feet as Joey folded and strapped the light rug he meant to put on Yarraman at night, arguing that a rug to a horse is worth an extra feed a day in the cold weather, and is much easier to carry. He packed what he could of light dry feed for the horses, but by and large he expected them to forage for themselves.

The sun was not even making its thin bright line of gold along the eastern horizon when Joey rode away from the shack with Yarraman snorting and blowing clouds of steam from his wide nostrils. The packmare followed and Reb and Wolf snapped and gambolled in the frost. Joey was warm in his rabbit-skin jacket, but his nose and eyes tingled with cold; he turned in the saddle and waved at his father standing on top of the hill, a tall, gaunt man looking like some stark, storm-swept tree that had been dried out by wind and sunshine until it had become almost indestructibly strong.

The packmare jogged behind Yarraman with a gentle creaking of leather and an occasional snort of warm steam from her nostrils. Joey felt like an Arctic explorer in his jacket, and he was glad of it, just as he was glad to feel the heat generated by Yarraman's big body warming his legs as they travelled along at a bush jog. He crossed the creek and rode round the foot of the mountain, across the plain, all the land that he hoped would soon be enclosed by the fence that was to be finished by the time he returned. He turned sharply east and felt that his journey had really begun.

The sun came up and the frost began to melt. It was quite warm now in the sunlight and Joey felt too hot in his hairy coat, but still when he passed through a clump of trees the shadows were very cold indeed, so he kept it on for a while longer. He rode over paddocks with no directions to follow, only knowing he must go east for half the distance and then turn southwards. Geoff's map did not begin until he had travelled a hundred miles or so.

He turned in the saddle and waved to his father

Reb ran about sniffing at every bush, and Joey felt gay and began to sing in his high boy's voice, while Yarraman, not to be outdone, curtseyed to an occasional shadow in a movement that was strangely light for such a coarse, powerful body. 'If only the weather keeps fine we'll make plenty of distance,' Joey thought to himself.

That night was the first time Joey had ever been away from the shack since his father had fetched him from the Children's Home in Sydney. He felt lonely when he had eaten the supper Rowena packed for him, and he stretched out on his water-proofed groundsheet and lay looking up at the stars, listening to the clinking of the hobbles on Yarraman and the mare. Reb came and stretched himself out against Joey's legs like a living hot-water bottle. A little distance away Wolf had dropped to the ground and was dozing with his long nose on his front paws. When Yarraman moved too far away in his grazing, Wolf rose silently, followed him and lay down again, repeating the pattern hour after hour all night long.

Jim missed Joey too. All day he and Geoff and Bill dug holes and erected posts. Rowena gave a couple of hours' hard work, and when they called it a day Jim was tired enough to welcome the thought of bed. But after his lonely supper, his work-hardened body recovered. He missed Joey so much that he walked over to the Bretts', chuckled when he found Bill still there, and they all sat around wondering what sort of a day Joey had had, speculating on how far he had ridden. When at last Jim rose to his feet to set off home, Rowena said,

'Jim, you can't work all day and then get a meal at night. While we're on the fencing, it'll be better if you all keep on half an hour longer then come back here together, and I'll have a hot meal ready for you.'

'Thanks, Rowena, but I wouldn't like . . .'

'Nonsense. That's settled. Feeding you three'll be my contribution towards Joey's fence. Besides, it's too lonely for you to go back to the shack now.'

'Too right it's lonely. Thanks, I'd like to come back here.'

It was late in the afternoon of the next day when Joey saw a dark line of trees that he knew meant a river or a creek in front of him. He rode down a fence towards it. Beyond the trees rose a thin plume of smoke smudging the sky, marking a dwelling of some sort. He decided to get round the fence where it must meet the river and to head for the smoke. From there he would get his bearings and the rations which every station owner gives the lone traveller. If it was a big property he would get meat, bread, tea and sugar; his father had told him never to miss a homestead because they would save him from carrying quantities of food in his saddlebags.

The fence dipped towards the creek. Reb was casting about ahead of him. He came running back, looking up at Joey, running ahead, circling again. Joey knew these tactics, there was something down there that Reb believed he should see.

Wolf loped off after Reb, and as Joey topped the little rise he saw the creek and on its bank a sagging, dilapidated tent. The wind blew against it, two of the tent-pegs were sprung, and it leaned there, an ugly travesty of a dwelling.

Joey called, 'Anyone there?' but there was no answer. He rode down the slope and swung off Yarraman's back a few feet from the tent. The packmare snorted and kept her distance. Reb peered anxiously through the drooping flap, but did not go inside the tent. It was a lonely look-

27

ing thing and Joey hesitated. Finally he went across, held the flap aside and peered in.

An old bunk stretched, sagging like everything else, along one side. The gum-leaves that had formed a mattress were scattered and blown about the earthen floor. Obviously the place had been deserted for some days.

Joey stepped outside and walked towards Yarraman. As he did so he caught sight of a small grey face peering at him from behind a tree. It was the forlorn face of a dog, and now he knew why Reb was casting about and was so interested in everything. He whistled softly, the face disappeared.

For a minute Joey stood thinking. He wanted to reach the building that made the plume of smoke before dark, and there was no time to fool about with someone else's dog. Anyway, if the dog was here, then the owner must be returning, he argued with himself, but he did not really believe a word he said. It must have been at least a week since anyone lived in the tent, and surely the dog had not been hanging about ever since then. The pathetic little muzzle peered from the other side of the tree. Joey moved towards it and it was whisked away. He sat down on a fallen log, then he remembered that there was a slice of meat in his saddlebag, so he told the dogs to 'sit', and went over to Yarraman and took out the meat. He went back and sat on the log again, talking softly, holding the meat out.

For a long time the sad little blue-grey face stared at him. Then gradually a small bitch, the smallest fully-grown 'bluey' that Joey had ever seen, separated itself from the tree. Joey put his hand on Reb, who crouched beside him, his whiskers twitching with interest.

Not only was it a small bitch, it was also in a pitiable condition of starvation. Joey kept very still and the bitch crept nearer. He noticed that one paw was badly mangled, as though the little dog had been caught in a trap. It limped its way forward, its famished eyes on the meat Joey held. Gradually its hunger grew too much for it; it rushed forward and fell upon the piece of meat.

Joey held on to the meat as the bitch pulled pieces from his hand, and his free hand went down on to the little animal's shoulder. It flinched, but the meat was too good to leave. With a firm, gentle hand Joey stroked the dog. He found a piece of dirty string tied too tightly round its throat. Very quietly he held the bitch and took his knife and cut the string. The meat was gone and the small bitch gazed askance at Reb, but Joey's quiet 'sit!' kept Reb in line. The boy bent down and lifted the bitch gently on to his knees, and examined the injured paw. The paw was healing, and it explained why, if her owner had left her for some days, she had not been able to catch her own food. Now that the ice was broken, the little dog snuggled close to Joey, who went on stroking and talking to her.

'What am I to do with you? I'm travellin', an' you can't run on that paw yet awhile. Anyway, what'll your master say if I take you with me? I suppose he'll come back for you sometime. Well, serve him right if he doesn't find you, leaving you in this mess. I tell you what we'll do. I'll carry you in front of me, what d'you say?'

Naturally the little bitch said nothing, but she looked eloquent love at Joey, who rubbed her head very gently. He picked her up, knowing that Yarraman would not mind. He often carried Reb in front of his saddle when they played some game or other.

Joey rode off towards the plume of smoke, with Reb, excited out of his usual calm, jumping up beside his stirrup to look at the blue bitch lying on the valise, and the packmare followed. Wolf had only taken the briefest interest in the small stranger and merely loped placidly along at Yarraman's heels. It was a misty evening when Joey rode up to a neat homestead, white and homely, set in a garden that was mostly trees, shrubs and climbing plants, with little grass, and criss-crossed by gravel paths. At the sound of horses' hooves and the creaking of saddle and pack, the boss came out, saying:

'Well, now what d'you want, young feller?'

Joey reined in Yarraman and smiled back at him.

'First of all, sir, do you know if this is anyone's dog? I found her near a deserted tent on the creek bank about three miles away. She seems to have had her paw in a trap; she's awful hungry.'

'Yeah, she's Morgan's dog. The old feller died about a week ago. My men found 'im, but they couldn't find the bitch. You'd better come on in, son.'

'Could I have a bit of tucker, sir?' Joey asked, making no move to dismount. 'I'm on my way to the mountains after some wild horses.'

'That wouldn't be the mob of brumbies my boys saw goin' through a coupla months ago? There were plenty white horses among them, goin' like dust-devils. If we hadn't been busy then we'd 'a bin after them.'

'Oh yes, that's Brumby's mob!' Joey said, then asked eagerly, 'Did you notice a fine white stallion p'raps following them? He's ours, he went off with them.'

'Can't say I did, but the boys might've. Who might you be, son?'

'I'm Joey Meehan. My Dad and I live next to Geoff Brett's place, Euro Downs.' He laughed. 'I guess our place is too small to have a name!'

'Come on, we'll git along to the stable. You can leave your horses in the yard tonight, we'll give you feed. I live here alone now. The cook'll find something an' give you a bit of feed for your dogs too.'

'Thanks very much.' Joey looked down at the little bitch and she looked back at him with nervous, imploring eyes. 'I don't want to put 'er down, she's nervous, might run away, an' she can't hunt yet with that paw.'

'Leave 'er here, one more dog don't make much difference to us. My lot're yarded back there, you can hear the noise.'

The little bitch shivered in Joey's arms.

'Thank you very much, but I think I'll take her with me, she's such a nervous little thing.'

'Please yourself, boy, but it's a bit of a handicap havin' to carry a dawg. I expect she had a pretty rotten life with old Morgan.'

Joey slid to the ground with the bitch held in the crook of one arm. He thought himself very silly to keep her. Even if she could run all right in a couple of days, she probably would not be much use to him. Reb put his paws on Joey's arm and the small bluey cowered against him. He squatted down, held the bitch on his knees and his hand felt the sharpness of her ribs under her loose skin.

'Here, Reb, gently now.' Reb licked her nose and Joey smiled. He knew that if she had been a male Reb would have growled and bristled and walked stiff-legged around them. He rose to his feet.

'She's terribly starved, Mr . . .'

'My name's Carroll, George Carroll. Yeah, I reckon she's more hungry than hurt right now. Come on to the back door. The cook'll give you a bit o' liver for 'er, better for 'er than beef right now. Then you can leave 'er in your room. I guess your dog sleeps there if I know dogs and boys!'

'Oh, thanks Mr Carroll, she needs some tucker.'

'Right, come on and I'll show you the kitchen.'

At the kitchen a round-faced Chinese cook gave Joey a

chunk of liver for the little bluey, and meaty bones for Reb and Wolf. Reb grabbed his bone and dropped it in the dirt, standing over it with bristling back, eyeing the bluey in a very unchivalrous manner. She busied herself wolfing the liver from Joey's hands and Reb, who was certainly not going to entertain any lady if it meant giving up his dinner, settled down to tearing and swallowing lumps of beef, strong paws on the bone, white teeth and bloodstained muzzle working hard.

Picking up the bluey, Joey and Mr Carroll walked along the veranda to the door of a small room. It was plainly furnished, and the boarded walls had been varnished so that the knots in the wood showed clearly, making strange faces and figures to fascinate Joey's eyes. Against one wall stood a plain iron bedstead with a heavy blue blanket folded at the foot. There was a window in the opposite wall out of which Joey saw the shadowy leaves of a eucalypt moving against the sky. A chair and a chest of drawers made up the rest of the furniture. A chintz curtain went diagonally across one corner and beneath it were hooks for clothes. It was a bare, plain little room, but comfortable enough for a boy, especially for one like Joey who had never seen a luxurious bedroom.

'The shower's at the far end of the veranda, Joey. Want another blanket, the nights're nippy?'

Joey shook his head. 'This'll do fine, Mr Carroll.'

The man nodded and went out of the door. Joey sat on the side of the bed and stroked the little bitch while Reb poked his nose everywhere and blew into the corners.

'Now you two stay here, and don't either of you make a noise.' He pulled off his fur jacket, put it on the floor and lifted the bitch on to it. 'There you are, Bluey – that's your name, girl, Bluey. Now you and Reb stay here while I have a shower. Sit, Reb.'

Reb watched these strange doings with sleepy eyes, and little Bluey cast adoring glances at Joey and whimpered softly as he went out of the door and closed it behind him. Wolf, as always, stayed with Yarraman. Theirs was one of those frequent, but strange, friendships between two dissimilar animals. Joey and Yarraman were the only two things in Wolf's life, and often through the night he would leave the horse for long enough to pad softly away to make sure that Joey was all right too. Having satisfied himself that Reb could be trusted to guard Jocy, Wolf always returned to Yarraman's side, and after the usual ceremony of nose-touching, a snort from the horse and a sneeze from Wolf, he would lie down for an hour or two before the same routine began again.

Joey, clean and comfortably tired, joined Mr Carroll and they went in to dinner. George Carroll enjoyed having a guest, and he liked boys of Joey's age, so that they got along well. There was a wood fire on the hearth, and after dinner the man and the boy sat in front of it. Joey was sleepy, but he struggled manfully not to show his drowsiness.

'Now, what about telling me why you're after those brumbies, boy? Why, you must be eighty miles from 'ome by now, and that's a long way for one boy and 'is dogs to be trailing a brumby herd, even if it's as fine a one as my men tell me passed this way a few months ago.'

So Joey told Mr Carroll how the brumbies lived on their mountain, and how his father, Geoff, Bill Regan and even Rowena were struggling to get the fence finished by the time he brought the herd back.

'What makes you think you'll be able to get the 'erd back?'

Joey looked straight into the kindly blue eyes opposite him and said simply,

'Reb an' I'll bring 'em back for sure.'

'What's your mother think of a nipper like you goin' off this way?'

'I haven't a mother, only Dad. Rowena's been like a mother to me. She's Geoff's wife; she used to teach school an' she's given me postal lessons ever since I was seven.'

'I wondered where you'd learned to talk so good,' Mr Carroll said with respect. His own schooling had been very limited. 'How long d'you reckon it'll take you to reach the snow?'

Joey thought for a minute before he said,

'Another three or four days, I should think. You see, I'll need Yarraman to be fresh when we catch up with Brumby's mob. Yarraman looks a bit clumsy, but he's really pretty fast and he's strong too.'

Mr Carroll nodded, 'Yes, I can see that. But I dunno, boy, you're takin' on quite a job.'

'I *must* do it, Mr Carroll.' Joey leaned forward and the firelight flickered across his earnest young face. 'Don't you see, they're *my* herd. I've waited for that fence Dad and the others're putting up all of my life. Brumby's mine, Dad bought him for me from a buck-jumping show, but I wouldn't keep him shut up. Besides, Moonlight and Florian are somewhere about, an' I don't know what Dad an' I'd do without Florian; he's getting known as a sire now,' he added proudly.

Mr Carroll smiled at him. 'Want me to send a couple of my men with you and some spare horses?'

Joey looked shocked. 'Oh no, thank you, sir, Reb and I'll manage – besides, it's better just to be me. The brumbies're used to seeing me about, and of course Moonlight and Florian know me well. If there were any strangers I'd never get the herd together to start them in the direction I want them to go. More'n likely they'd

stampede and I mightn't get them together again. I'd like
you to look at my map and to add anything you can
think of to help, if you will, please?' Joey held out the
paper Geoff had given him.

'Right.' George Carroll stretched out his hand and took
it. 'If you won't let me help you, son, I'll tell you what
I'll do. When Florian's at stud again I'll send over some
of my mares, maybe come along myself and have a look
at how you an' your Dad're gettin' along?'

Joey's face shone. 'Oh, will you really, Mr Carroll?
That'd be great. Dad'd like to meet you an' you'd like
Florian if you saw him. He mightn't have a pedigree in
the stud book, but he's a real champion, you come and
see.'

They spread out the map. Mr Carroll turned it over
and drew a careful map of the west side of the Mountains, marking any features he could remember, putting
a cross here and there where he thought a brumby herd
would be likely to graze.

'There're often a couple of small mobs up there pinch-
ing each others' mares and fighting for leadership. Right
'ere,' he put his finger on the spot, 'you'll find a hut an'
Bruce Merry. Tell 'im I sent you.'

Joey looked worried, but he said nothing and he forgot
Bruce Merry. Mr Carroll said good night and sent Joey
off to bed. As he opened the door Reb jumped up at him;
he was not used to being away from Joey. Little Bluey
thumped her tail and put her paws on Joey's knees as he
sat down on his bed to pull his boots off. He fondled her
head with his left hand and with his right pulled Reb
over to him, talking to both his dogs, telling them of all
the work he expected them to do in the next few
weeks.

He lifted Bluey's paw and saw how healthy it looked,
and decided she could run a little the next day. He

wondered if she would be much help, and decided that with her breeding she must have inherited some knowledge of rounding-up any four-footed strays that might come her way.

He lay back on the bed. The mattress seemed strange to him; all his life he had slept on a mattress of gum-leaves, gathered fresh every few days. He missed the aromatic scent of the leaves as the weight and warmth of his body pressed them down.

Through the window the three-quarter moon seemed to be chased by dark, silver-selvedged clouds across the sky. Reb was restless and finally Joey motioned him on to the foot of the bed where he settled down, sure that any move that might take Joey away would waken him.

Joey was too excited to sleep at once. He lay there and thought about how he had first seen Wolf on just such a moonlit night as this, when he and his father had wakened to fierce squealings and neighings from behind the stable. There, in the light that turned every object to frosted whiteness, they saw Moonlight rear up, her sharp hooves driving downwards at a gaunt dog that was trying to get at her foal.

In all the excitement they thought the dog was a dingo, and thought that it was very strange for it to attack a foal. The thin, powerful dog slipped away with the dingo's faculty for silent movement, blending with ground and bushes. Jim and Joey took Moonlight and the foal back to the stable and shut them in. Then they went back to bed.

Next morning, Joey told Rowena all about it when he carried over the milk, and stayed on at his lessons.

'Poor brute,' Rowena said. 'It might be old Saltbush's dog, you remember him, the old swaggy that comes this way every couple of years. He died in hospital about a month ago, or so Geoff heard, and he had a half-Alsatian, half-dingo that disappeared. It could easily've turned killer.'

After that, apart from making sure that Moonlight and her foal were safe, Joey forgot about the killer dog until one day when he was walking up from the creek he heard a gasping sound and a rustling of bushes. He went to look and saw a yellow-grey dog lying on its side, its ribs pitifully sharp. It tried to scrabble its way to cover while one dreadfully swollen foot was held in a cruel iron trap which it had evidently torn from the ground and dragged after it for many days.

The poor emaciated creature glared at him with eyes of fear and hate, but Joey could only feel compassion for it and a wish to help. He tore a strip from his shirt and went near to it. It dragged itself around to face him, snarling hideously. Joey tied the creature's jaws together with the strip of shirt, then, with one foot on the cruel iron trap and with the whole strength of his hands, he opened the jaws and released the paw. He examined it; it was badly injured but the leg was unbroken. He tried to pick up the thin body in his arms, but the wild thing fought him, wheezing and growling with utmost fury. So Joey tied its legs, being very careful not to hurt the injured paw. He managed to lift the emaciated body in his arms and finally reached home with it.

Staggering into the shack Joey put his burden gently on the bed. Then he tied the exhausted but still furious creature so that it could move a little, but not escape. His own supper, a piece of steak given him by Rowena as his father was away for a couple of nights, Joey cut into four pieces and then he went back to the snarling dog. Its jaws were untied, and as Joey held out the pieces of raw meat long strings of saliva drooled from its starving jaws. It was obviously desperate with hunger but it would not eat from alien hands.

With infinite patience Joey persuaded it to eat. The growling and the fierce red flickering of the eyes died down except when the boy came very near, then they started up again. Joey filled a tin dish with water and put it where the dog could reach it. He knew that if, having fed, it would drink, then it would proceed to clean and lick its own wounds so that healing could start.

Having done all he could, Joey made his greatest sacrifice for the fierce animal he had rescued. He took down his father's gun and did what he hated to do, he shot a rabbit so that the starved one might have the fresh meat and blood it craved.

That night the dog lay on Joey's bed while he slept on his father's. For a long time after its wounds healed the dog still growled and glared at Joey. Jim said 'give it up, that half-dingo'll have to be destroyed. You'll never tame it, and you can't let it go. It's got all the Alsatian's cunning along with the dingo's savagery; it's a real killer. Better let me do what's best now, Joey, and don't go breaking your heart over it.'

For a long time Joey refused to give up, then very sadly one evening he went round to where the untamed creature, which he was sure had belonged to old Salt-bush, lay glaring at him. He squatted before the dog and it growled. 'It's a pity you have to die because you loved your old master and won't love me,' Joey told it sorrowfully. The dog bared its teeth.

Joey put out his hand, the swift, snarling jaws closed on his wrist and blood trickled from the broken skin. The boy did not pull his hand away and the dog looked at him uncertainly, then dropped his wrist. Joey went calmly on with its feeding. When the food was gone he undid the collar and chain, then without looking at the wild creature again he walked away. He knew his father would be angry, but he would not deny the wild dog its day or two of freedom. It was well-fed, it would not kill until it was time for it to be killed.

Feeling sad and defeated Joey walked out beyond the stable so that he would not see the dog disappear. He stooped beneath the fence and walked across the stubbly grass to where Yarraman grazed. Yarraman lifting his head, whickered at him. Joey ran his hand round the shaggy head, getting comfort from the clean smell of the horse's hide, leaning his head against the young Yarraman's rough neck.

Something bumped against Joey's legs, a cold nose was thrust into the hand that hung idly at his side. His heart leaped; moving quietly he looked down into the eyes of the killer dog. Those eyes were no longer baleful. They looked steadily up at Joey, and the red tongue came out as if the dog was smiling at him. Joey squatted on his heels, and the dog leaned confidingly against him as he rubbed its once-savage head and talked to it.

'So what you needed was to be free, that was it, eh? Are you my dog now, you wolf-dog, you? Wolf! Yes, that's it, that's what I'll call you.' The young Yarraman bent his long neck and snorted at the dog. Wolf licked the horse's nose, and that began a fast friendship in which only the boy was allowed to join, although Rebel was eventually allowed a certain measure of their companionship.

His remembrance of how Wolf came to him having reached its pleasant conclusion, Joey turned restlessly on the mattress that was strange to him and Reb opened a sleepy eye. Soon they were both fast asleep.

Joey wakened at daylight. He went towards the yard where Yarraman moved about, and as he passed the kitchen the round moonface of the Chinese cook looked out at him.

'You velly early, but big Boss around, you catchum blekfus' plitty soon now.'

Joey thanked him and went along to where Mr Carroll had told him to take feed for Yarraman and the pack-mare. He rubbed down both of his horses and pulled feed-bags on them. The little Bluey and Reb sniffed about the yard, and Joey was glad to see that her limp was improving. She looked fatter too, in the way of a dog that is a good doer, and immediately uses up the food it eats. He looked up and Mr Carroll waved to him from the fence. They walked back to breakfast together. The sound of thudding hooves and the shouts of the men bringing in a bunch of saddle horses came across the crisp air.

'That's Dave bringin' in the stock horses,' Mr Carroll remarked, and the horses came into sight driven by a slim half-caste boy.

After breakfast Joey said good-bye. Mr Carroll insisted on his taking the heavy blue blanket from his bed.

'You don't know how badly you might need it in the Mountains, son,' he said as they walked down to the yards together. The stockmen were saddling their horses and Mr Carroll introduced the boy to them. The men looked at him curiously when Mr Carroll told them that Joey was after the brumby mob that had passed through a couple of months before.

One man, tightening up the girth, his face against the saddle-flap, turned his head a little and grinned at the man next to him. Joey caught the look and flushed. Obviously the men did not believe he would be able to take the herd back to his home mountain.

He rode off after thanking Mr Carroll very sincerely for all his help and kindness. His young jaw was set hard as he disappeared into the distance, his slim boyish figure tall and dark against the sky from Yarraman's big back, the packmare jogging behind him. Standing looking at his receding back one of the stockmen said,

'E's got Buckley's chance of gettin' that brumby mob, eh Boss?'

Mr Carroll turned his shrewd eyes on the man.

'Could be, Thompson, but I dunno, I've got ten bob that says the boy'll be back, mob an' all, inside of a month?'

'Done, Boss! It's a shame to take the money!'

After he had travelled three or four miles Joey dismounted and lifted Bluey on to the front of his saddle. She had been running well, but he thought she had had enough. She put her head up and licked him under the chin and they rode on. The air became cooler. They did not pass any more homesteads, and when they stopped for the night Joey was glad of his rations and of the blanket Mr Carroll gave him, glad too, to sit near his small fire while he ate. The two horses moved about grazing on the dry grass, and Joey spread his groundsheet, and with a dog on each side of him he went off to sleep.

Joey had never before been more than fifty miles away from his home since the day Jim brought him back with him to a complete change of surroundings.

In the morning he went carefully over his two horses, looking at their hooves, making sure that no weakness in them would betray him when the crucial time arrived. Bluey appeared almost plump; she was a pretty little bitch and Joey looked at her fondly, and Reb certainly considered that she was his property and that he had rescued her himself. Joey hoped that the time would not arrive when Reb and Wolf might fight for her favours.

Their way led upwards now, up long slopes down which the cold air blew from the mountains. Then the smooth, upward-tilting plains were broken up by rocks and stunted timber, and the ground fell away steeply, making two sides of a deep crease in the earth where a clear, cold creek ran. Joey was very glad to wear the rough rabbit-skin coat of his and Rowena's making. He began rugging his horses at night, and though the rugs were thin and light, the horses appreciated them. There was another reason why Joey wanted his horses rugged, a reason that applied more to the packmare than it did to Yarraman. If Brumby or any other wild stallion attempted to drive off the mare in the darkness of the night, the rug would make the stallion cautious. It would be strange to him and make him wary of it and so keep him away from the mare.

The uphill drag was tiring. Joey slackened his pace a little; it was not worth saving time and tiring out his horses. Days that had been clear and sunny, with sparklingly cold air, now changed. The sky darkened as though a great asphalt-coloured awning stretched over it. It had a louring, stormy look and Joey, who was interested in every strange leaf of grass, every twisted tree, guessed that a storm was brewing. He had no way of knowing how long it would be before the storm struck, nor of its severity, but he tingled with excited anticipation, and with impatience too. If the storm was anything like the pictures in Rowena's old encyclopedia, then it might blot out the distance and delay his search.

It was early dusk, and the purple darkness swallowed up the last stretch of daylight when, on the steep slope of a small gully, he saw a sturdily built wooden hut with a smoking chimney.

Part Two

As Joey's horses' hooves rang out on the hard stony ground, a man came to the door and looked out. He cooeed to Joey. The boy turned Yarraman's head and the big horse went down the hillside with proppy, sure steps that jolted Joey so much that he let Bluey slide down his leg from her perch on Mr Carroll's blue blanket where it was rolled across the pommel. He had carried her for the last five or six miles, and she was delighted at feeling the hard earth beneath her paws again and dashed off after Reb.

There was a sudden movement behind the legs of the man in the doorway and a big yellow mongrel pushed his way out, growling ferociously. Joey called Reb to him in a high, anxious voice, but he was too late. The big dog had seen the little bitch and she circled wildly away from him, running towards Reb for protection. Joey yelled at his dogs, the man in the doorway shouted at the mongrel, but now Wolf bounded forward and the two dogs glared at each other over the slim blue back of the little bitch. They were deaf and blind to anything but the wild instinct that drives rival dogs to battle.

Joey, telling Reb furiously to 'sit', sent Yarraman hurtling down the slope with the surprised packmare following. The man took a couple of limping steps from the doorway, but by then both dogs were walking stilt-legged around each other, growling like far-off thunder, lips drawn back and teeth gleaming in wolf-like snarls.

Apart from his fear of harm coming to Wolf, Joey knew that Reb would join in, and should he be lamed then there would be no chance of finding the brumby herd and of bringing it home. Bluey, her soft eyes troubled, ran to Yarraman's side and Joey slid to the ground, pulling the reins over his horse's head. He stooped and picked up Bluey before he hurried towards the fighters.

Joey was conscious that the badly-limping man in the doorway of the hut had disappeared inside again and for a second he felt furious that he was making no attempt to stop the fight. 'It doesn't matter to him,' Joey thought angrily. 'He isn't trailing wild horses with only his dogs to help him.'

Then the man appeared carrying a bucket of water in his hands and Joey knew that he had wronged him. He hurried down the hill and Reb rushed by him. He shouted angrily, but the half-wild dogs were deaf to human voices, listening only for the pitch and menace in each other's snarls, seeing only each other's flame-lit eyes as they circled warily for the all-important first grip. Reb's dingo blood sent him driving in low at Wolf's side. Before Joey or the strange man could reach them a struggling, hurtling mass of hairy bodies were locked together.

The limping man did his best, but handicapped as he was he could not reach the dogs in time. Joey sprinted to his side, snatched the bucket and threw the water as hard as he could at the dogs. The effect was instantaneous. The icy mountain water so surprised and shocked the fighters that, gasping and panting, they sprang apart.

Joey seized Reb by a neck-fold, and the lame man did the same with his dog. Wolf looked around in complete surprise. He was shivering with cold and his enemies had melted away! The three formidable fighters were just

Joey snatched the bucket and threw the water at the dogs

cold, drenched dogs who were rather sorry for themselves.

The boy and the man caught each other's eyes and grinned. The man hauled his sopping dog towards Joey, who pulled Reb over. They rubbed their wild heads together and not even a growl broke the silence from the shivering creatures.

With his tail between his legs the sorry-looking mongrel followed his master into the shack, and the man returned to the door, threw a piece of rough towelling to Joey and said,

'Come on in, rub your dogs down with this. There'll be no more fighting, I've tied my bloke up. Come on in, it's cold out there.'

A glance showed Joey, Yarraman and the packmare plucking at stubbly grass sprouting between the rocks and he put Bluey down, grabbed Reb and Wolf and dragged them just inside the hut. He gave Reb a thorough rub-down. Reb looked up at him sideways and Joey said 'You old fool, don't you start fighting, you're my best man.' His arm went round Reb's neck and Reb licked his cheek while Joey mumbled, 'I can't spare you.'

Then he gave Wolf, who sat looking both cold and apologetic, a brisk rub and he shook himself and trotted off to find Yarraman while Joey smiled and said, 'You're an old fool too, you'd be much warmer in here!'

Bluey, sitting on the sidelines, tilted her head this way and that, her bright, gentle eyes taking it all in. After another brisk rub Joey let Reb go and he sprinted about outside, taking nature's way of warming himself up. Joey's face was anxious; if Reb sickened even the least bit, the handicap would be a heavy one. He glanced around the hut, conscious for the first time of the bright wood fire and the lame man who knelt in front of it and rubbed his dog so that its coat steamed. Joey whistled

Reb back to him, and with his hand on his neck went towards the fire. The bearded man looked up, holding the towel on his dog, and asked,

'Everything's O.K., isn't it?'

'Yes thanks, Reb's fine. Wolf, my other dog, won't leave Yarraman. That bucket of cold water was a new experience for my dogs. I hope they didn't hurt your dog, mister?'

'No, the silly old coot's in one piece, bit of a slash in his flank but that'll soon heal. The bitch comin' around was too much for him.'

Joey nodded. 'Reb thought he was going to lose his girl, I suppose, an' Wolf loves a scrap anyhow.'

The man led his dog to a corner and fastened him to one of the inner posts.

'Get your dog before the fire, he'll dry off better. The bitch'll be all right in here now.'

Joey said gratefully, 'Thanks very much, mister. Reb's pretty important to me any time, just now I couldn't do without him. I'll get him dry then we'll be on our way.'

'No fear, not tonight. It's goin' to storm and you wouldn't get far, so it'd be better to stay here. Where're you making for?'

'Up into the mountains, but thanks, if you'll have us tonight we'll be glad to stay. I've never been in a snow-storm so I don't know how bad it might be. I'll warm Reb up a bit and then see to the horses. I've got tucker in my bags, and feed for the horses and the dogs.'

'Leave it there. I've got plenty of meat. The station sent out darn near a whole sheep yesterday. It'll keep this weather, but not all that well; I'll be glad to be rid of some of it. Anyway one of the hands'll be along next week with more meat. I keep my eye on the cattle that go too high up here, but I hurt my leg last week and I haven't been able to do too much since then. I'll be glad of company if it really snows. You might be stuck here a coupla days. How about your horses, are they used to it?'

'No, none of us are. I brought light rugs for them, they'll help a bit, I expect.'

The man nodded. 'Thought your horses looked a bit short in the hair for these parts. If the rugs'll keep out the sleet they'll help a lot. Bring your gear inside here, it won't be much good to you if the leather freezes up – an' how about your other dog?'

'He won't leave my horse, Yarraman, you know how it is.'

The man nodded. 'There's an empty packing-case and a bit of a lean-to at the back of the hut. Tie your horses out there and they'll miss the worst of the weather, and here – chuck this old blanket on to the straw in the packing-case and your dog won't freeze either.'

Joey thanked him and went out where the air was dark and there were no stars beginning to glimmer in the sky. It seemed to Joey that a great purple-grey blanket was suspended a few feet above his head; the wind whistled around with an icy, keening noise. The horses were just blurs in the distance, and with Reb and Bluey at his heels Joey went off and got them, bringing them to where a wedge of lamplight fell across the rough ground in front of the open door. He pulled off the packs and saddle, rubbed the horses down and put on their blankets. Then he led them round to the shelter of the lean-to and tethered them there, putting on their feed-bags and giving them a small feed from the stock which Mr Carroll had replenished for him.

The horses munched away contentedly and Joey gave them a pat, and cast a doubtful look at the sky. If the wind did not change they would be fairly well sheltered; if wind and snow blew into the lean-to, like all horses they would want to turn their rumps to the weather, so he left their halters long enough for them to move about a little.

Dragging the big square wooden case nearer to Yarraman, Joey turned it on its side, shook up the straw that was in it and wedged an edge of the old blanket into a wide crack. Then he whistled Wolf to him. He showed his dog the case and patted the blanket, saying, 'Get in there, boy.' Wolf inspected the whole thing carefully, then stepped gingerly into it, turning round as his wolf-dog ancestors had done, finally settling himself with a contented sigh, head on paws, eyes on the large blur that was Yarraman. Joey gave his gaunt head an affectionate rub and left him.

Whistling the other two dogs to him, Joey pulled the door to behind them. He felt his luck was really in to lead him to such a cosy place for the stormy night, and he said so to the herder, who told him his name was Bruce Merry. Then Joey remembered and told him that Mr Carroll had said to find him. The dogs pushed close to Joey, delighted with the warmth that was reaching out to them from the flames; the big mongrel lay watching them with surly, surprised eyes, these interlopers were taking his place by the fire.

Bruce was delighted to have a visitor, and Joey who had not 'travelled' before reflected what a nice world he lived in. People were always pleased to have you drop in, to offer you food and to make you comfortable for the night.

Bruce looked at the boy with shrewd eyes and made no comment when Joey told him of his quest. In spite of the untrimmed beard and rough clothes, Joey realized that his host had more education than anyone he had met before, except perhaps Rowena. On one side of the hut there was a well-filled bookshelf, with so many books in it that some of them had been thrust sideways on top of the upright rows. He longed to look at them, but he did not feel it would be polite.

After they had warmed themselves Bruce brought a big feed of meat for each of the dogs. He threw a lump of meat and a bone to his own dog, then handed the other portions to Joey, who fed Reb and Bluey from his hands, in the way they liked best. Finally each dog, including Wolf, got a big bare bone and settled down contentedly chewing the gristle and licking away at the little plugs of marrow that blocked each end.

'You like dogs?' Joey asked as he leaned against the door to close it again after feeding Wolf, and Bruce nodded.

'I do. I like dogs and horses and kids with guts like you have, kids that go off to do a hard job on their own without whining for anyone to help them.'

Joey flushed with pleasure and said,

'But I've had a lot of help. Mr Carroll helped me a few nights ago, and now you've taken us in – an' I'll tell you, Bruce, I was a bit worried about what a storm'd be like up here, I've never seen snow, not even really bad sleet in my life.'

'Well, that sort of help is give and take, you didn't come looking for it, and there's nothing wrong with using any luck that comes your way. I like the lonely life up here, that's why I took it on, gives me time to read, but I like company sometimes, I can tell you, and I was pretty glad to see you ridin' in.'

They talked for a while and Bruce saw Joey's eyes straying to his bookshelf.

'Go on, take a look,' he told him, 'they're all about the sort of things I'm interested in, and not everybody's meat. But there's quite a bit of lighter stuff. Take a look around while I get the tucker.'

Joey stood entranced in front of the bookshelf. He had quite a library himself, one that he and Rowena had built up during the years they had been together. Most of Joey's books were concerned with horses in one way or the other. Bruce's books were a varied lot; there were books about the sea; Westerns with thrilling covers that Joey gazed at with awed eyes, horses as beautiful as Florian, as savage as Brumby, and men riding them in fringed trousers and buckskin shirts; books about parts of the world that were only names to Joey; and others, books of poetry, and one big book on veterinary surgery. Joey's excitement mounted.

'May I look at this one?' he called.

'Surely, take out any books you want.' He broke off; a loud whistling howl sounded about the little hut. 'Listen to that! That storm's workin' up, you won't have much to do except read for the next coupla days by the sound of it.'

Joey held up a paper-back with two great white horses rearing against each other ridden by men with long spurs and gay neckerchiefs.

'What's this?'

'That's a Western.'

'You mean it's about cowboys and things?'

'Are *you* a scrubber, son! There are thousands of Westerns written by blokes that've never seen a muster. Some aren't much good, but that one isn't bad. They're about America in the early days when the cowboys and the Indians rode and fought and lassooed mustangs, the wild horses the Spaniards left behind them down Mexico way.'

'Oh, I know about *them* – the mustangs I mean,' Joey said in rather a shocked voice, and he sat down to read his first Western. Although for the last half hour he had felt ravenously hungry, that was forgotten and he was almost sorry when Bruce called him to get his plate and tuck in.

From an oven that looked like a biscuit tin, Bruce took a shoulder of roast mutton which Joey thoroughly enjoyed. There was something about being in that little hut, warm and fire-lit while the storm raged outside, his animals safe and well-fed, that added to the thrill Joey got from reading his first cowboy book in between discussing his own mission with Bruce who told him all he could about the mountains, and where he thought would be the most likely places to find his herd.

Later on, rolled in his blanket on the floor, Joey read his book by the flickering light of the fire, so that when he finished it he also had to come back from a world of vast plains dark with buffalo herds sweeping like great black clouds across them; from a world of Indians and brown-faced pioneers in fringed jackets and carrying guns in a land where their horses often meant their lives; and to remember that he was in a little hut on the lower slopes of mountains he had come to search, that he too had wild horses to conquer and work to do.

For the boy who had never been away from his bush home before, whose acquaintances were few and his friends not many more than the four loved ones about his home, the Western opened up new worlds, gave him a realization of other lives than his own, other places he had never known before.

Joey lay thinking to himself of kindly George Carroll, of his warm welcome from Bruce, of the niceness that perhaps awaited him from hundreds of as yet unknown people that were outside his secluded life, and for the first time he felt a stirring of wanderlust. Places, people, a whole world of them were waiting to be discovered. To the screeching of the wind that buffeted the hut and sometimes flattened the flames in the hearth as though

they were in brief bondage to the screaming hosts outside, leaping up as each great gust spent itself, the boy
dropped off to sleep.

Stinging sleet rode on the wind. Yarraman and the
packmare huddled together, sheltered by the sturdy
wooden wall and watched by Wolf who, made restless
by conditions he did not understand, came out of his
improvised kennel to lick the stinging sleet off his long
grey nose, sniff at Yarraman, circle about in the fierce
driving wind and eventually return to doze in his box
again, his strong body warm within the coarse grey hair
of his coat.

At dawn the wind died down until it mewed about the
hut and then stopped as the snow began to fall, white,
silent, mysterious. Joey slept on. When he woke Bruce
was already up and replenishing the fire from the big
stack of logs that filled one corner of the room.

'You've never seen snow, Joey, so now take a look
outside.'

Joey jumped to his feet and Bruce called,

'Hey! Not so fast, put on your skin-coat or you'll
freeze.'

So Joey dressed hastily while Reb bounded about him
and sleepy-eyed little Bluey snuggled into the blanket he
had warmed with his body. He unlatched the door and a
gust of wind snatched it from his hands and blew a cloud
of ashes from the fireplace as the boy slipped hastily
outside with Reb beside him and hauled the door to. Not
until then did he look about him. On his upturned face
small flakes of snow fell lightly, overhead the sky was
leaden, but the atmosphere was warmer than when the
sleet was falling.

What excited Joey were the patches of snow that lay
about the ground in their pure whiteness, a whiteness
such as he had never imagined. 'It's as white as my

Moonlight,' Joey said to himself. Actually it was not much of a snowfall, it was not an unbroken sheet of incredible whiteness covering the ground, but just a few inches of snow lying in the hollows with a layer spread over the hut roof and along the tops of the branches of twisted trees, but to Joey it was fairyland. He bent and took a handful from the drift by the door. It sparkled and slid through his fingers, leaving his hand damp, and he looked at his palm in wonder for having held such miraculous purity. Reb was almost as awed as his master. His early morning dash landed him in a snow-filled hole and he floundered out in great astonishment.

Joey went round the back of the hut and his horses whinnied when they saw him. He stroked their heads, tugging at their ears as he talked to them, and then decided to leave their rugs on a little longer. Wolf came out of his kennel and gave Joey his usual warm, but rather grave greeting. He regarded the snow with great suspicion, and Joey stooped and gathered up a handful of the delicious stuff, and landed a snowball gently on Wolf's long nose. Wolf sneezed, and looked his disapproval of such goings-on; then he decided that if his world was going to change like this he might as well enjoy it. He set off with his long, loping strides after Reb. As Joey turned back into the hut he saw his two dogs, chest deep in a drift, snapping at the mysterious white stuff and kicking it over each other. He smiled to himself and went indoors.

'It's marvellous, I wish Dad could see it,' he told Bruce, who said,

'You wait until there's a real snow-storm, this one's only playing at it. Still, the weather looks pretty chancy and I think you ought to stay here until it settles one way or the other. That way you'll give your horses and dogs time to get used to cold.'

Joey hesitated, he so much wanted to read more of Bruce's wonderful books that he searched his conscience to be sure it was not just self-indulgence that was trying to divert him from the trail of his horses. He frowned and did not answer at once. Bruce smiled, he knew what that hesitation came from.

'Look, Joey, if you insist on leaving before this storm settles I'll have to go with you, I won't let you go alone, but I don't feel much like moving about on this leg, so be a good bloke and don't make me do it. Stay another day or two. You'll get there just as fast in the end, and you'll all know a lot more about snow-conditions and what to expect if you get stuck in a blizzard higher up, than you do now.'

Joey knew that Bruce was talking sense, and he gave a quick breath of relief.

'O.K. You know this country an' I don't. I'd like to stay very much. I'd better go and take the rugs off the horses, and let 'em move around a bit to warm themselves. Actually they can do with a spell. I want them at their top when we catch up with Brumby; he's really fast, and he drives his herd fast too. I don't know how Florian'll be, he's never gone wild before, but if I have to rope him he'll certainly extend Yarraman.'

'Remember this, if you can't get a horse with bursts of speed, you'll always get him in the end if you've the patience, just by following wherever he goes, even if it's on foot. Why, in one of those books in my shelves you'll find the true story of two brothers who went after mustangs on foot. They followed for so long they ended up thinking they were wild horses themselves! When one of them was roped by a cowboy he tried to pull away just as a horse would – anyway, it's that red book at the end, read it for yourself.'

During those two days Joey learned more about the

world outside his home than he had learned in the rest of his young life. He read hungrily, varying Westerns with books about the sea. From these books he got some idea of the power and majesty of the oceans, of tides and storms moving with the rolling of liquid thunder thousands of fathoms below the surface, gathering power until the mighty ground-swells became the white-topped demonic waves of the surface, mountainous slopes of water fringed with frothing whiteness like the manes of giant horses.

He read far into the night by the flickering flames of the fire. It was a library of adventure, and Joey dropped off to sleep, his heavy lids falling over eyes filled with the colour-tinged brilliance of glare-ice, of polar bears at evening, their great bodies orange from the rays of the setting sun; ice-floes cracking when the giant killer whales bump their noses under a floe to dislodge a dozing seal, or pop up like huge black-and-white corks around the edge to see if their prey is still there.

Once Joey woke with a yelp like a hunting dog, and explained to the startled Bruce that he was dreaming he was in a small boat when from the horizon of his dream raced a gigantic killer, its powerful body glistening between the watery walls made by its speed, wallowing and plunging with all its terrible power.

Worlds about which he had no conception registered themselves in his mind for future study. But when he took the big book on veterinary practice, he forgot these other worlds and sat absorbed in his study of all the ills that might happen to a horse, trying to remember the symptoms, the care and the cure. Even the Westerns were forgotten. Bruce was both pleased and touched by the boy's avid desire to learn. In between reading, Joey attended to his animals, helped Bruce about the hut and for hours they talked together. The two days seemed to Joey to pass in a flash.

As Bruce guessed it would, the storm blew itself out, and on the third morning Joey woke early to clear skies and sunshine and decided regretfully that he must pass on.

'Come in on your way back, if you're passing here,' Bruce told him, but they both knew that he could not choose the exact direction the mob would take. He hated to leave Bruce's companionship, the warm hut and the many unread books. As a farewell present Bruce handed him two unread Westerns.

'These won't take up too much room, but fill those saddlebags of yours with all the meat, dry feed and stuff you can get in them, you won't find much in the feed line for any of you high in the mountains.'

Joey looked at him earnestly. 'I don't know what I'd've done if you hadn't been here. I see now I wouldn't't've got far with the tucker and horse-feed I began with.'

Bruce agreed. 'Put that down to something you've learned; knowing what you'll need is the basis of all good expedition-planning. Come on, let's have breakfast and then you'd better get on your way. The snow'll be thicker higher up; you're most likely to find your brumbies in some valley, high up, but not at the very top of the range. Then your troubles'll begin, but good luck to you anyhow.'

So Joey left his second friend with his mind still full of new worlds, shining worlds of glaciers, emerald seas or steamy green jungles. These worlds were on paper; around him was a part of his own homeland, and it was a new world too, a living world.

Joey rode along at an easy pace, and his horses were as excited at this new world as he and his dogs were. The boy looked at the dark, twisted trunks poking sparsely leaved tops above depressions filled with the white purity of untouched snow. Bruce had told him what to expect in the way of grass and trees, and he recognized the first straggling, springy snowgrass growing in grey-green tussocks. He passed trees he recognized as eucalypts, with straight white trunks rising above him, and he wondered if they were the manna gums about which Bruce had also told him.

The winter scene held no wild flowers; the small streams were clear and icy-cold, flowing over metallic-looking bottoms. He watched the sky anxiously but it remained clear. He meant to follow Bruce's advice, ride high up and then begin to spiral the mountains downwards.

As the evening came on the snow deepened about them and the setting sun threw a pinky light across its whiteness. Joey looked anxiously about him. He must find a sheltered spot for the night and he realized that he did not really know what sort of shelter he should watch for. 'I've been spoiled,' he thought to himself, 'I've lived too easily between Mr Carroll and Bruce.'

He rode on peering about him and saw a big granite rock overhanging the ground below. The top was like a roof heavy with snow, but beneath it he saw there was shelter for his animals and himself. He rode towards it.

The ground beneath the overhang was dark and clear of snow. He moved his horses in, rubbed them down and put on their feed bags, then walked up the slope and gathered an armful of fairly dry sticks and broken branches and hurried back with it. He detached the small tomahawk from his saddle and broke and chopped some substantial pieces of the bigger wood with this, and built his fire. He had an anxious moment wondering what he would do if the wind changed and drove under the overhang, but decided that was all in the luck of the game.

Joey rugged his horses, called the three dogs to him and examined their paws. The rest had completed the cure of Bluey's paw, and all three dogs were in fine fettle. He hobbled his horses and untied them once he was sure they would know where to find shelter and left them to nose industriously at the layers of snow, occasionally pounding it with impatient hooves. Joey saw that if they were hungry enough they could get a feed from what grass there was providing they worked for it, and he decided that he must husband most of his dry feed for later on when there might not be enough available grass.

The boy felt small and lonely in his strange surroundings, perched on a harsh mountain-side, but he built a fire, put the larger pieces of wood near by to add to it through the night, fed the dogs and himself and then spread out on his bed and resisted the temptation to read one of his Westerns. They too were emergency fodder to be used to divert his mind when they were most needed.

Joey was asleep almost before he felt the two dogs snuggling against him. Reb lay along his legs, but little Bluey liked to creep into his arms or snuggle against his back, and he was glad to have her warm little body against the icy air. Overhead his last glance was up at the frosty stars that gleamed against a cobalt sky.

By the next evening Joey felt he was as high up the mountains as the brumby herd was likely to come. The sky was dark and louring again and he felt troubled. The cold was such that he was glad that through Bruce's wisdom he and his animals had had time to become a little acclimatized. He found a smaller overhang that night, a place that was more like a little cave carved from the icy cold of the granite outcrop.

The storm struck in the early hours of the morning,

and the grey, uncertain light showed Joey a world that was more thickly white than any he had seen before. He saw too his first real snowfall. Instead of the tiny flakes he had seen before, these flakes were large and fluffy, descending in a curtain of whiteness that blotted out the world ten feet away, and which somehow made the boy uneasy by its soundlessness. There was something he felt was unnatural about this steady downward drift of broken whiteness that kept up continuous movement but without a whisper of sound.

He rose to his feet and was relieved to find the horses, their rumps to the weather, huddling under the ledge a few feet away. He realized that if they had not been there he would have had little chance of finding them in the silent, blind whiteness about him. He tethered them in case they might want to move away, but left the tethers long enough to let them move out a little and search for grass tussocks, and he resisted the temptation to give them a feed. If he did this then they would not learn to forage, and they must learn. He told himself that if they did not get a reasonable amount of picking by evening then he would give them each a small feed. He was thankful that Bruce's generosity had supplied him with enough food for himself and his animals for several days if need be.

In spite of his fur jacket, Joey was shaking with cold as he moved back into the little cave, and he added a few sticks to his fire. He had no idea how long this storm would last and they could not go on until it stopped snowing.

After two nights and a day Joey felt desperate. If only the steady downfall would stop; until it did he could not find a direction, his map was useless and there was no chance of sighting the herd. He was worried about their rations, they would not last many more days. Then suddenly the snow stopped falling and it began to freeze.

The cold before was nothing to this; if he had no other goal its intensity would still have started him moving. The going was rough. Joey walked ahead of his horses, floundering into the deeper drifts, worrying that they might break a leg over a hidden rock or in some snow-filled hole.

The movement and the struggle to get out of the many holes warmed him. Now the clear air allowed him to get a rough bearing from the careful map of the mountain ridges that Bruce had drawn him. He set his course around the slope of the mountain on which he found himself. It pleased him that the dogs never seemed to notice the intense cold, they floundered about, chased each other and came periodically back to him for approval throughout the long and difficult day.

That night he could not find an overhang or a cave. He thought that the driving snow had probably filled in beneath the overhangs so that he could not tell where they might be. This meant that night, for them all, must be spent in the open. The still cold was bad enough, he prayed that the blizzard-like wind would not sweep across them.

Joey stopped in a bleak grove of what he thought must be half-a-dozen snow gums, twisted shapes with their barks patterned in many faint colours, reddish tinges interspersed with greens, grey and yellows, and some of them were a good size round the boles. There was one from which a limb had been torn. By crawling under this he found a little shelter where the bole was hollowed and he decided that, cold as it would un-doubtedly be, this slight shelter would be better than none.

Digging and piling the snow, the boy made a high bank around him, and he sat back and felt rather pleased with the results. Although the curious, floundering dogs kept plunging across his wall, breaking it down, there remained plenty of material for rebuilding, and their scrambling merely packed the wall more tightly and helped its impenetrability.

The dogs were enchanted. They rushed about through the snow, paying Joey visits every few minutes as he carried his wind-break along against the trailing limb. Against this he intended to tether his horses.

It was almost dark; he laid his fire in a cleared space when Wolf came leaping over the wall with a furry body in his mouth. This was a large whitish-grey rabbit, and Joey felt glad that here was at least some food which his animals could catch for themselves. He took it gently from Wolf's savage jaws, and was glad when he realized that the grim snap had ended the little creature's life instantly. Joey took out his knife and cut the rabbit into three, giving Wolf, the provider and the dog with the largest frame to fill, the major portion. Then he whistled up the other two and fed them. He thought how fortunate it was that he had taught Wolf to bring his kills back to him, so that he might share them out. Joey was always glad when his dogs foraged for themselves; he disliked killing rabbits himself when they fell so swiftly to the dogs' own jaws.

He tethered Yarraman against the branch, right next to the walled hollow he had made, and hoped for his own as well as for Wolf's sake he would come into the hollow and sleep there with the other dogs. Above him he would be able to see Yarraman's shaggy dark head.

The night was freezingly cold, but the closely packed snowy walls kept the wind away, and all three dogs slept against him. Wolf made several excursions, making a breach in the snow wall each time he went to satisfy himself that his beloved Yarraman was safe. On the whole it was far warmer than Joey had thought it would be.

The next morning broke bright and clear with a shining beauty that was new to Joey. The real search for Florian and the herd began. The slopes of the mountain were not over-steep, studded occasionally by out-crops of granite rocks, and never quite treeless. The snow, which on steeper slopes would have been inclined to move downwards, was nowhere much more than a foot to eighteen inches deep, and often barely covered the ground. Nevertheless it remained a scarcely known world to the six beings who circled the mountain's frosty face.

Joey thought often of his father, of Geoff and Bill, but most often he thought of Rowena, and he wondered how he would have fared if she had not given him the thick socks and warm gloves that he found so comforting.

Far to the north-west his father and friends thought of Joey too. He had been gone a fortnight and they still toiled on with the fencing. They found it necessary to make a detour and that meant felling more trees and hand-cutting the posts from them. Then these posts had to be dragged to the proper places, as for years they had been slowly dragging the other posts, and left to weather even if only for a few days. All this meant delay, but while they did not slow up on the work, no one quite believed that Joey, with or without his brumby mob, could be back within a month.

Of course Rowena worried most about Joey; the men realized he might have to put up with cold and hunger and other hardship just as Rowena knew it, but this knowledge tore at her heart even more than it did at theirs.

The sunlight was mellow on that crisp winter's day as Rowena moved about the house and dreamed about Joey. A sudden warm, fragrant smell from her oven sent her back to the kitchen to take a batch of sweet scones from its warm interior. She rolled them in a spotless kitchen towel, and put the bundle in an old sugarbag in which she had already placed beef sandwiches and a jar of pickles. She swung the rough bag over her shoulder and her tall, gaunt figure crossed the veranda and started out towards where the fencers were hard at work three miles away. She always took them their lunch, it saved time. Once there she helped to fence for a couple of hours, then trudged back to get an evening meal ready for the hungry men.

The only thing that worried Rowena more than Joey's being away was the thought that he might arrive home before the fence was finished. As she tramped across the hard winter earth she turned her head and looked eastward; somewhere nearly two hundred miles away, Joey pursued his quest, alone except for his dogs and his horses. She knew him so well, he had been to her everything that a son might have been since the time she overcame his shyness with the boy-bait of hot scones and honey. He had been such a small frail boy, not much higher than the kitchen table. And as long as she had known him he had had this dream of 'his' herd; Joey's dreams were not the sort that melted away when the going became tough. He had gone serenely on towards his goal, contented to work and to wait. With all her heart Rowena hoped that life would give him what he wanted – and that when it was his he would still want it with that same single-minded intensity.

Ahead of her Rowena saw Jim's long back bent over a post-hole while opposite him Geoff held the post steady. With their rough boots they began to kick the earth into the hole and stamp it down.

'Hi there!' Rowena called, 'Sorry I'm late, but the wood was green and the oven wouldn't heat.'

The three busy men hailed her and went on with their jobs while she gathered the sticks and lit the fire. She picked up the blackened billy standing against a fallen tree where the men's coats had been flung over the rough bark. Rowena went down the steep bank to the creek and filled the billy and went back and put it on the fire. The little flames crackled around it, turned to pale, ghostly wisps by the sunlight.

Jim straightened up and stretched his cracking muscles; he and the others joined the woman, perching themselves like great drab birds along the tree-trunk, munching contentedly at the food she had brought, swallowing it with mouthfuls of the billy tea from their tin mugs. Rowena stopped eating and asked in a questioning way,

'I wonder what Joey's doing right now?'

Geoff grinned at her. 'You're always saying that, I believe that in your mind you've gone every inch of the way with Joey!'

Jim reached over and took one of the scones; it was still warm and he bit into it appreciatively. 'I think the boy's just about reached the mountains by now. He said he'd be there in a week, I thought then more'n likely it'd be two weeks.'

Bill agreed with him and Rowena sighed, 'It seems such a long time. I wish we could see him riding in from over there.'

'Hey!' Geoff interrupted her. 'Don't wish that until the fencin's done or we'll be in a hell of a row!'

The others smiled and Rowena agreed. 'All the same, if it was right now I'd be glad. Joey's never been away before, I – well I hate it.'

For four days Joey travelled around the mountain, peering about him, but finding no sign of Brumby's herd, and no sign of Florian. Next morning, he got his pack together, his hands fumbling through his thick gloves. The temperature had fallen in the night; he shivered at the sun's light dimmed by thick clouds as the raw sleet blew against his chapped face. He stood with his two horses beside him, when he heard the faint echo of a neigh.

Joey dropped his valise, and ran up the ridge behind him because it hid the downward slope of the hill beyond. The dogs raced with him. Reb reached the top first and looked into the distance quivering with excitement. Just as Joey reached Reb he tripped over a snow-covered root and pitched headlong on to his face. He scrambled to his feet and peered into the distance.

On the far slope five black dots were showing; they were horses all right. Joey studied them. He knew the lines of every horse in Brumby's mob. Four of the horses beyond, he thought, were mares, and the bigger, rangier horse he supposed would be the stallion. It trotted round its tiny herd, nipping the slower mares on the rump. They were certainly brumbies, but they were not any part of Brumby's herd; the stallion was a big bay, and not of Brumby's quality. All the same the mere fact that at last he had seen brumbies on the hills cheered Joey. He went back, tied on his pack, mounted Yarraman and set off.

Day was darkened by the clouds, a little sleety rain continued to fall as the horses crossed the iron-hard earth that was thinly covered in a sheet of snow, their hooves rang on the ground as if it had been metal. The ground was freezing hard.

That night was the coldest one of all, even the dogs huddled, rather miserably, close to the boy. In the morning the greyish light showed him that the wind had blown the loose snow about and the ground was still as hard as iron. Yarraman and the packmare dug the sharp edges of their hooves vainly into it, trying to smash through to the edible stuff beneath. After a time of digging and snorting they got a few mouthfuls; the dry feed that Joey carried was so low that he dared not give them more than a handful each.

The boy's life had been spent on arid plains, where in summer the hot winds scorched the grass and the pools of water dried inwards until nothing was left but hard grey mud, cracked and bleached by the sunshine, hot as newly baked bread. Now at least they were untroubled by the need for water. Sometimes the little mountain streams were iced over; often he put snow in his billy and melted it so that both the dogs and the horses could drink it.

Joey himself was tiring; he felt weary and impatient, but he never thought of giving up. He was living in one of those different worlds that interested him intensely. As long as he felt the need to strive, he was alive in the sense he appreciated. He remembered two lines he had read in a small green-covered book of poetry he had found in Bruce's shelves, and which he had read just as avidly as he had the more adventurous prose :

> Clay lies still, but blood's a rover;
> Breath's a ware that will not keep.

Joey liked that; its words came as near to expressing life to him as words ever would. He thought of this and of the other pages he had read that made specific impressions on him, as he turned back and mounted his horse. He thought rather longingly of his precious Westerns. He had not even peeped inside their covers, they were to be a reward when the job was done.

As he rode along he tried to think of anything but the intense cold that was bedevilling him. At any rate he consoled himself with the rather doubtful comfort that at home his people would have plenty of time to finish the fence before he returned.

A cruel, cutting east wind blew against them; once Joey was so cold that he dismounted and walked, swinging his arms and stamping his feet to get some warmth into his body. His breath came in clouds of steam and he tried to whistle through his chapped lips. They moved across a mountain-face which was covered in scattered rocks and big granite out-croppings, and the going was slow and difficult. The hungry horses wanted to stop continuously to dig through the snowy ground between the rocks where, Joey supposed, lush grasses had grown in the springtime.

Numbed with cold, the boy was riding when he heard the sound for the first time. Across the icy air came a clinking, metallic noise. He turned in his saddle, thinking that perhaps the packmare had struck a rock with her shoe, or had stumbled on the iron ground. But she was close beside him. Again – the clinking rang out through the mountain air.

Joey reined in Yarraman and listened intently. He looked around him; the three dogs had heard the strange metallic sound, all were alert in their different ways, trying to pin-point the direction of the noise. There was silence. Reb turned his head more into the wind, little Bluey trembled with the excitement of the unknown; Wolf stood, the unmoving savagery of his head silhouetted against the sky like that other Grey Brother who had also loved a boy. It came again, three times, the clanging noise followed by a muffled grunt and a sliding sound.

Joey felt sure the noise came from downhill, and apparently the dogs agreed with him. The three streaked through the snow as Joey turned Yarraman's big head down the slope. He wondered if it might not prove to be some mountain bird that made a cry like clinking ice, just as the coachman-bird of the plains had a cry like the crack of a whip.

Yarraman went downhill with a certain caution; he was becoming used to making sudden slides on the glassy down-slopes and he always recovered himself, but he was rather like a beginner on skates, not yet quite sure of himself.

Again the noises came, followed by a snort of weary exasperation. Then Joey knew that somewhere out of sight a horse was struggling to move. Perhaps it had fallen on the icy slope, or was somehow caught in the rocks.

Joey sprang to the ground and pulled the reins over Yarraman's head. Immediately the big horse joined the packmare nosing for feed, and their stamping and snorting blotted out the other sounds.

Joey followed the dogs forward, walking cautiously. They climbed a big pile of rocks, their jagged tops sticking through the white coverlet. All three dogs began a silent stalking, heads down, shoulders moving like well-oiled pistons, and the boy followed. A curtain of snow fell from a rocky outcrop, for this was the weather-side of the mountain, and beneath the snow a black crevice had formed. The dogs went towards this. Whatever made the noises was somewhere beneath that cheerless curtain.

The dogs moved a few feet, and stopped, raised their heads and looked at Joey. He decided that, breast deep in the snow the wind had driven from the upper slopes, they had stopped because the ground was treacherous. To the dogs' disappointment he moved away to where a stunted snowgum grew and wrenched a thin, straight stick from it. The dogs moved restlessly as he came back and began moving slowly forward, feeling his way with the end of the stick.

Now the silence beneath the rock was broken, there was a clattering of hooves, snorting and neighing. Joey stopped, not knowing what to do. A horse was somewhere down there below him, but how could he reach it? The prodding stick went into nothingness, and Joey put his foot forward until it too was suspended in space. He leaned forward and began to scrape at the overhanging snow, wondering what could be holding it like a roof across the crevice.

Scraping and tugging he came on the skeleton of dried branches and leaves that had once belonged to a tree that had fallen, dried and become a kind of lattice work on which the snow had built up into a lengthy covering.

Now that he knew what it was, Joey moved back a few paces and thought hard. Obviously before he could help the imprisoned horse he must pull away the snow and the branches until he had enough light to see how deep the cavern was.

He turned back and the dogs looked disconsolately after him. He mounted Yarraman, and with the dogs following he rode down to where he could look up at the projection and its sparkling curtain. Yes, obviously the whole thing depended from the old stump farther up the mountain. He rode Yarraman back near the stump, then dismounted and lifted the coil of raw-hide from his saddle. He left Yarraman and walked to the old stump and tied the raw-hide firmly around it. Then allowing the necessary amount of rope he pushed himself gently forward until he was right on the edge of the overhang, made a hole with his stick and looked downwards.

Below him he saw a whitish blur about three or four feet beneath. He pushed the snow away around him, bar-ing the spreading vine of grey boughs that roofed the icy cavern beneath.

Joey was troubled. This was a new problem which he felt he must solve, he could not leave any horse in that terrible position; it was impossible to tell how long the poor brute had been there already. At least it was alive, but in the end, if he could not help it, it would suffer a terrible death.

He undid the rope from around himself, bent down and began to dig the snow away from the stump. Its roots clutched octopus-like at the hard earth. It was old and crackly with no boughs on the upper side, but the 'roof' boughs were still attached to the mother-stump. Joey dug, kicked and pulled, scratching and tearing at the hard earth with his numbed fingers so that some of it came away from the roots.

Then he returned to Yarraman and took his tomahawk from his saddle and chopped with that. Below, he could hear the restless movements of the horse, its small snorts and heavy breathing. 'Poor beast,' he thought, 'I hope I can get you out.'

When he had removed as much earth as he could so that the feeble old stump was loosened, he straightened up, and bringing Yarraman nearer he fastened a loose end of the rope to the cleats on his saddle. Then he patted Yarraman, saying,

'Come on now, old fella, we've got to help that bloke down there somehow or other.'

He led his horse quietly up the hill and the rope tightened. Yarraman pulled steadily and the old stump creaked and groaned. Yarraman planted his big hooves firmly and pulled with his powerful shoulders. The stump moved. Again – it moved a little farther and a shower of dry sticks and snow fell on to the imprisoned animal. It stamped and snorted its fear as its restless back became covered in the cold rubble.

Pulling steadily Yarraman slowly drew the stump from the ground, its roots and its long arms spread like a fan behind him, away from the overhang, up on to the snow beyond. Joey patted his horse. 'Good boy, you've done it.' Then he untied the two ends of the raw-hide. The dragging of the stump followed by its tangle of dead arms had cleared everything away that had obstructed their view of the horse and which had kept it in the cold and dull light below. The dogs stood on the edge of the overhang and Joey went to join them. Reb was obviously excited, he whined ecstatically; Bluey was merely astonished and Wolf growled and rumbled in his big throat.

Joey advanced carefully and peered down. Below him was a cave-like crevice, its walls hard, smooth, frozen and about seven feet high. At one end the vertical side became a slope. In the centre of the crevice, its back covered in rubbish, stood a big silvery-white horse that, given a run-back, could have soared over such a barrier, but as it was, it was hemmed in so that it could not turn. It had plunged forward a thousand times in the past sad, frustrating days, only to slide back down the steep, slippery slope. It was the noise of the helpless hooves beating and dragging at the ice that had caught Joey's attention.

He stared down at the poor beast, unable to see it clearly because of the narrowness of its prison. Through the lumps of snow, the twigs and grassy little tussocks on its back he could see that it was a big white horse. Just then the restless, frightened beast, trapped so hopelessly, reared up a little and its front hooves beat against the terrible sloping wall ahead of it; it twisted its head on

Its front hooves beat against the terrible wall ahead

its long neck and peered upwards out of eyes ringed with the white of fear. Joey cried,

'Florian! Oh, Florian, I've found you!'

The stallion's helpless hooves slid back but it threw up its splendid head and neighed wildly.

'Florian, steady boy, don't worry, I'll get you out!'

Joey scrambled down the side of the rock and walked to the sloping end of the icy trap. He could not reach his horse, but the fear went from Florian's eyes and he whickered at his master. Joey did not know what to do, but he refused to let himself be gripped by despair. Somehow, 'if I have to dig one end out with my bare hands, frozen earth an' all, I'll get you out,' he told his horse. But how could it be done?

He thought for a while, squatting on his heels and talked softly all the time. He knew that whatever he decided to do, Florian would fear and resent it, and it would be harder to help a frightened, angry horse than it would a calm one. So he talked on softly and reassuringly, moved round the side and leaned over and moved some of the rubble from the broad white back, and his heart contracted with pity as he saw the thin ribs raking from those once-splendid sides.

Florian looked as if he had been in that terrible living tomb for at least a week. Joey could see how he had plucked and torn at the sides for the lichen that grew there, and how the continuous rearing and pounding of his front hooves had scored the glassy slopes ahead of him. Only Florian's great heart that refused to give up had kept him alive. Jammed in as he was, the rearing and lurching at the slippery wall ahead of him was the only exercise he could manage. It kept his blood moving, and in his starved condition he would have frozen to death without movement.

Joey made up his mind. There was only one thing he

74

could do, drag Florian out as he had made Yarraman drag the stump from the frozen earth. He would have to rope him to Yarraman, and to do that he must go down into that dreadful hole himself.

It was just as well that Joey had brought such a length of the raw-hide rope that he and his father always made from their hides. Without this Florian would have been doomed. If he tied the thin, incredibly strong ropes about Florian his weight would make them cut into his skin, so he decided to go down to Florian carrying his saddle, and to tie the ropes to that. If the girth held he believed that Yarraman could get the stallion out.

Joey walked over to the big horse and removed the saddle. Then he roped himself to a piece of jutting rock; if that rope broke, then he would suffer the same fate as Florian. The whole prospect was very frightening. If Florian was upset by his sufferings and grew excited and plunged about when Joey landed in the icy box with him, Joey might be pounded by those mighty hooves or crushed against one of the hard cold walls, but however he tried to think of some other way there did not seem to be one. He had to risk it.

With the saddle across one arm and the raw-hide held taut in the other hand so that it would slide through his palm as he lowered himself slowly, he put his feet over on to the icy downward slope, speaking quietly to Florian. The boy knew that Florian was actually his greatest danger. Then he eased himself down the slide as slowly as he could manage it, blessing Rowena in his mind, for without the stout woollen gloves his palm would have been raw.

Florian took small restless steps, undecided what it was all about and whether he ought not to plunge once more in an effort to get out. Joey spoke to him firmly and he stood still, his intelligent eyes on his master. Joey felt his feet touch the bottom, Florian's head was above his own. The space was so cramped that the saddle was pressed against the horse's chest.

Joey let go the end of the rope that was tied around his waist and put his hand up to Florian's head, stroking him and whispering to him. Florian bumped his head up and down and knocked Joey against the wall. At first Joey could not see how he could get room beside Florian to lift the saddle on to his back, but finally he managed it. Then the raw-hide ropes had to be fastened to the cleats. He ducked under Florian's big body and raised one leg after the other by grabbing the fetlocks, and arranged the ropes the way he wanted them.

Pushing himself upright, with the loose ends of the ropes tied to his own waist, Joey stood fondling the horse, trying to quieten him, and finally letting him find the handful of dry feed he had put in one pocket for him. The famished horse pushed and nudged at it.

Suddenly Joey knew that he had made a ghastly mistake. That mouthful of feed had not calmed Florian, on the contrary it had raised all the demons of food-craving within the big body. Florian was almost frantic with hunger, and as the boy tried to pull himself up by his own rope Florian squealed and butted him, trying to get his nose back in the pocket that had held the one wonderful, delicious mouthful of real feed.

The furious bumping knocked Joey back to the trampled earth of the cave and he fell to the ground under those great hooves. He literally climbed up Florian's leg in his efforts to clamber up the wall and Florian shook his head furiously, squealing and nipping at Joey's left arm. The boy felt the grinding teeth meet on his skin and he gasped and flinched. Florian backed and moved about in the few inches he could manage; the wild look had come back into his eyes. Through the pain of his arm Joey saw with dismay that the horse was snaking his head at him with flattened ears, and the wild dark eyes were ringed by the tell-tale fear-circles of white.

Now Joey knew real fear himself. It seemed that both he and Florian were doomed to a ghastly death in that icy pit, and all through the one small mistake of the handful of feed he had brought, meaning to comfort and calm his horse.

Joey flattened himself against the wall and gripped the rope, but those bruising teeth had taken the power out of one arm. Florian gave the high squeal of an angry stallion, which is a terrifying sound, but still, even in the madness of his hunger, he did not attack Joey. Joey's other great fear was that the raw-hide ropes might get tangled, or would snap beneath the powerful, restless hooves. He thought he had just one chance.

He squeezed himself along the left side of the slippery wall, and the excited breathing of the huge body pressed against him almost crushed his own ribs, but, with a few inches of space on either side, Florian's quickly-moving hooves next pushed himself against the far wall. Joey saw his chance and he took it. Somehow, in spite of the helplessness of one arm, he pulled himself upward, and with one light spring he was in the saddle.

It seemed that Florian imagined himself ridden by an enemy, he squealed and reared and Joey, risking everything, left the saddle and sprang to grip the rocky top of the wall. If he fell now he was doomed, the excited horse would trample him to death. Under his clutching arm he saw the horse rear upwards and try to twist his head to grab at Joey's legs. The solid teeth were bared, the ears back, a great savage demon was just below him, trying to pick him off the slippery wall, a creature gone temporarily mad from hunger, cold and hardship. But the terrible snaking head could not quite get round to seize him. Trembling with weariness and dreadful fear Joey hauled himself up and rolled out on to the snow.

He longed to lie there for a moment to recover, but he knew that if Florian twisted the raw-hide ropes tied to Joey's own waist, he would be pulled back into that cold tomb from which he had only just escaped. Trembling a little, Joey got to his feet, his face twisting with the pain of his bitten left arm. 'Lucky the bone didn't crack,' he told himself.

Anyway, he had climbed out of that dark and icy tomb and his dogs were greeting him joyfully. Yarraman stood patiently waiting for him, as if he understood that his beloved master had taken about all he could stand, and Joey knew he had better get on with the business.

With rather shaky knees he walked over to Yarraman and undid the ropes that bound him to Florian, straightened them and fastened them to the harness he had improvised for his stalwart old friend. Joey was not at all sure how Florian would behave once he was out of his prison, if he could be got out, but it would be a very serious thing if he did no more than gallop off in his freedom, carrying Joey's saddle with him.

Still, that was just one more risk the boy knew he must take. 'Yarraman, thank goodness I have you,' he whispered with a little break of pure misery in his voice. Now that the moment had come the thought of failure was uppermost, but he forced it back. He remembered thankfully that he had broken Florian to the saddle himself, and in the doing the boy had taught the colt one or two of the tricks he read about in Rowena's encyclopedia, which had two pages devoted to the training of the beautiful Lippizaners of Vienna.

When Joey called 'Hup!' to Florian, he had taught him to leap forward, and he prayed that he had not forgotten that particular trick now, when he must call to the horse and have his voice obeyed, now when the intelligent eyes could not even see him.

Having fixed the ropes he walked back to the sloping end of the evil crevice and spoke soothingly to the horse. Florian jigged about, but the high, mad excitement seemed to have left him. Joey went back to Yarraman saying, 'Come on, old feller, gently now!'

It was one thing to expect Yarraman to pull an inanimate stump out of the earth; that he could understand, but it was quite another to find himself on the other end of ropes that held him to what might very well turn out to be a struggling demon heavier than himself. Florian *must* be persuaded to help himself. With his heart in his mouth Joey led Yarraman a few steps until the ropes drew taut, then he turned and shouted,

'Florian! Hup boy! Hup!'

At the same time he led Yarraman steadily forward. There was a great tattooing of hooves, then Joey walking backward and holding firmly to Yarraman's reins saw first Florian's great out-thrust hooves, then his head as the stallion strained against his lissom traces. Another pull. 'Oh God, don't let Florian fall back!' One more step – the stallion's chest was dragging on the ground, he lurched to his feet as a trace snapped, he was out! He had been saved from a living death and he stood there, his legs spread apart in his weakness, and looked with wondering eyes at the world about him.

Florian bent his head and blew against the snow, then he lifted it and came in a rather unsteady walk towards Joey whose own knees were shaking so that he had to force calmness on himself to meet his horse.

They met, and Joey's one good arm went round Florian's neck. He buried his nose against the solid flesh that was cold to the touch, and a salty tear burned its way down his chapped face. Florian whickered gently and turned his head to nibble at Joey's neck as he had always done.

Because of Joey's care there were two small feeds of dry stuff left. Yarraman and the packmare had become adept at digging up snow-grass, and while they could have done with more feed they were not too badly off. Joey decided that Florian's need was greater than theirs; the two feeds would help the stallion back on his feet again. Joey went to where he had piled his gear, put one feed in a nosebag and brought it back to Florian.

With his freedom all the madness and terror went from the stallion. He ate eagerly enough, poor starved brute, and sunlight that lay like a pale stain over the landscape seemed warming to him by contrast. After a time, as he stood munching hungrily, the marble-coldness of his flesh gave way to warmth. When he had finished his feed Joey took his nosebag off, and Florian began digging in the ground, tearing at any grass-blades or tussocks he could uncover.

Joey went back to look for one last time down into the horrible trap below the rock. He did not like leaving it open, but there was nothing else he could do, and he rather suspected that, if it had been open, then Florian might not have fallen into it. He looked into the gloomy dampness, the glistening of the walls, and he supposed that at least Florian had been able to get moisture from the horrid trickles which were the fruit of his own once-warm body. It was a terrible place, and Joey turned away quickly and went back to finish unsaddling Florian and resaddling Yarraman. In a day or two, if Florian picked up as he hoped he would, he would ride him alternately with Yarraman. In the meantime he would keep him on a lead. The thought of losing the stallion again was not to be borne.

So the little procession started on its way once more on the hunt for Brumby and his mob. Now that all the fear and uncertainty over Florian was at an end, Joey felt that he had at least accomplished half of what he had set out to do. Supposing he had not come to the mountains? He shuddered and refused to think about it.

Florian proved to be pitiably weak, so they did not go far that day. At nightfall Joey rugged him with the blanket Mr Carroll had given him, and prepared himself stoically for a chilly night. Apart from becoming a little acclimatized, Joey had learned a great deal about making camp and keeping warm in the snow. His arm was swollen, but he could do nothing much about it, not even look at it without getting very cold. It felt as if it must be badly bruised at the very least. He considered his injury a small price to pay for having Florian returned to him.

In its way, the stallion's weakness was all to the good. He would become civilized again by the time he returned to his full strength and speed, and be manageable in the old way.

That night was a happy one for Joey. No personal pain, no coldness could blot out the fact that Florian was back with him again. It was a very happy boy who fell asleep.

In the morning Joey found Florian sprightly beneath his warm rug, but he was not yet his magnificent self. Even the two small feeds had made his ribs less obvious, and had given him the stamina to dig vigorously for more food. It was the hefty ring of his hooves on the ice that woke Joey. The dogs were up and about, except Bluey, who never left her place at Joey's back until he got up. The gentle little bitch could do with all the love and fondling Joey had time to give her.

Joey learned that the smaller the hole he made in the snow, the warmer he was through the night, so he managed to make a space that would exactly fit himself and the dogs. He turned on his back and put a hand on Bluey's head. She opened her soft dark eyes and snuggled closer. Joey lay for a few minutes making a decision.

He had Florian, would it be best to turn back and go home? He weighed the question, but somehow, sensible as the idea might be, he could not make up his mind to give up yet awhile.

Horses, dogs and boy were fit but thin. The horses did remarkably well on such feed as they could get for themselves, and sometimes they mumbled at the bark and the sparse leaves of the trees. There were enough rabbits about, and the three dogs brought their kills to Joey, who was thankful that they were not as heartily sick of the taste of rabbit as he was himself. Still, it kept the warmth in his body. The rabbits were bigger than those he knew, their ears were smaller and their paws had pads of strong, springy hair between the toes so that the occasional prints as they hopped across the snow were fuzzy-edged, unlike those of the home rabbits which he had seen small and clearly defined at the muddy edges of creeks. Joey pondered about the small ears, the whitish-greyness of the fur and decided it was to do with living in the snow. The furry padding on the paws he supposed kept the skin-surfaces of the pads off the ice.

He decided to go on. He had been away for eighteen days, he would give himself another week to search in; if he had not found the mob by then, he would turn back and take Florian home. His father would be satisfied if he got the stallion back, but he, Joey, would he be satisfied that he had done his utmost to find the brumbies? He knew that he would not.

The searching began again. Each evening Joey rugged Florian a little later and removed it earlier. He was glad to have it for the stallion when he was weakened by confinement and starvation, but once the horse began to pick up his splendid strength, it would not be necessary.

Day after day they took their winding way around the mountain. Joey rode Florian alternately with Yarraman. Florian was already becoming imperious, bossing Yarraman, nipping the mare, inclined to drive them both ahead of him as is the way with the master of a mob.

Joey rode Florian one afternoon, passing beneath a ridge of blackish rocks poking above the snow, while all around them was a smooth snowy slope broken by a few trees. Ahead of them plodded Yarraman and the mare, and the boy gazed lazily into the distance, longing to see moving dots on the far slopes that might be horses. The slopes spread before him, broad and white and empty under a grey sky.

Their spiral descent had taken them quite a long way down the mountains and Joey had to force himself not to lose heart. He glanced around and saw the dogs, all three of them, muzzles in the air, standing quite still with their black noses moving and sniffing. They were gazing up beyond the ridge of rocks and Joey reined back Florian, who flung his head in the air and gazed wildly about him.

Now Joey heard the sounds that mystified his animals. Shrill whinnies came nearer, then the thud of hooves through the thin covering of snow. The next instant, round one end of a ridge of rock a herd of horses came flooding down; grey horses and brown ones, wild horses whose coats had grown shaggy in the cold; the hard winter feeding had given them condition without fat. Their manes tossed wildly and their eyes shone in the clear air.

Florian needed all Joey's attention. The packmare backed towards the overhang, but Yarraman, driven to wild excitement by the whinnying and pounding of hooves, whinnied himself and reared, shaking his massive head.

On came the wild horses pouring round the overhang before they sighted the boy with his horses and dogs. Then they veered away, plunging downwards on to the broad white slope below them, and last of all came a splendid, silvery stallion, his beautiful head held high, galloping freely as he turned and twisted, covering his herd from the rear. He squealed at the laggards and nipped the mares' rumps if they dared to slow up.

It was Brumby. Joey gave a gasp of joy as he held

Florian from joining in the wild gallop. The stallion was afire with excitement and the boy fought to steady him. Ahead he saw Yarraman plunge among the galloping horses with Wolf at his heels, and the already swift galloping of the herd increased in pace.

Joey knew that in the glimpse they had caught of him, the herd did not connect him with the figure they saw so often near their mountain home. Given time to steady down he believed they would remember him. The packmare moved restlessly back and forth, but she did not go after the herd and Joey was glad of this. Reb trembled with eagerness, waiting for Joey's command to go after Yarraman, but Joey did not give the word. He quietened Florian and rode on the trail of the wild horses while the dogs and the packmare followed.

Yarraman, a gelding, running with the herd, was not in danger from Brumby. If it had been Florian who had gone after them he and Brumby would have fought to the death for command of the herd. It was obvious to Joey that soon after Florian broke out to follow the herd he must have picked up two or three mares which constituted a herd of his own, so that in following Brumby, and yet keeping his mares to himself, he had arrived at the point where he was trapped, and in all probability the deserted mares wandered off and eventually found their way into Brumby's, or into another stallion's mob.

To Joey the big herd was old Brumby's, and it would remain that way as long as he was able to keep it so. He let Yarraman go, and to keep complete control of Florian he would ride him during the day and hobble him at night. If he really needed Yarraman then Reb and Bluey would bring him out of the herd.

Joey was hot and on edge from his brief struggle with Florian, but nothing could dampen his spirits; he had found his herd. In a day or two the mares would be used to him and there would be no tendency to stampede when they saw him. Gently, day by day he would push them in the direction he meant them to go, leaving Brumby the illusion that it was his own choice. He was so happy and excited that he sang an old song that Rowena had taught him as a little boy:

> 'There's some as ride like sailors do
> With arms and legs and teeth,
> There's some as ride on top their horse
> And some ride underneath.'

The snowy slope stretched before him. Curved through it was a wide swathe disturbed by the hooves of the wild mob. Sometimes, where Brumby had nipped a mare and made her wheel, the thin snowy covering had been screwed away and tiny patches of dark earth showed; the rest was like a cake that has been topped by icing too hard to set smoothly, but to Joey it was the most beautiful sight in the world. He forgot his injured arm, and the fact that he would probably have to go on eating rabbits for another couple of weeks. All he knew was that on the roughened snow ahead of him, touched to shiningness by the pale sun, was the trail of his own, his splendid herd, and whatever the difficulties, he was going to take them home.

The boy rode along steadily and after about five miles he could see that the herd had slowed up. Then they wheeled to the right, and half a mile farther on he reined in Florian, who saw what he saw and jigged excitedly. Below them on the scrappy snow of the curve of the hill that rose from a small clear creek, the wild horses stopped to browse. For the first time they were not just an indistinguishable flood of rumps and backs. Joey's heart leaped with joy. In the middle of the herd was the little silvery mare, Moonlight, Florian's dam. The boy saw her rather halting gait that never seemed to reduce her speed when she ran with the herd. Florian, Brumby, Moonlight, all his lost loved ones.

He could see Yarraman's big dark form on the outside of the herd, and Brumby, who trotted continually round his harem, ignoring both Yarraman and Wolf whom he knew so well, and who did not count in his continual watchfulness against danger.

That evening Florian was hobbled and tied on a double lead. He was restless, whinnying frequently, following Joey with his intelligent eyes, but neither resentful nor rebellious of his shackles.

From the foot of the mountains the country would be strange to Joey, but he decided that as Brumby had brought the herd safely through it, he had the best chance of getting them home – if only he could be sure that Brumby meant to go home! He noticed that some of the mares would foal in the spring. They would be anxious to go back to the place of their last foaling, but that instinct for return would not touch them for several more months; it was useless to rely on them.

Moonlight was one who always came home to foal. Sitting there, his arms clasped about his knees, looking like a shabby crouching bear in his rabbit-skin coat, Joey remembered the time he had heard Moonlight whickering in the scrub at the foot of the brumbies' mountain, and of how he had gone to her and there she was, nudging her new-born colt, a smoky little fellow, who got to his small hooves, swaying there, legs spread wide for balance, tiny hooves firm on the earth – Florian, Brumby's son.

He turned his head to where Florian dug away at the snow with powerful hooves, getting hard-earned feed. Joey's loving eyes watched the power and beauty of the animal.

For five days Joey followed the herd, sleeping a little closer to it each night. Without really frightening them, his presence had disturbed them. As they fed, some impulse born of their leader would strike through them and the whole herd would plunge ahead, galloping and wheeling. Joey followed their broad trail in a leisurely way, stopping when they stopped. All the same their tactics worried the boy, but he did not worry much as long as Brumby continued to drive his herd towards their home mountain, and so far they were going in that general direction.

On the sixth day he decided that by now the herd were once again used to his unpressing presence, and that the time had come to take control. The day's riding, in spite of continual stops when the herd spread out to feed, was tiring because of Florian's excited pulling. He seemed to have all his vitality back again after the drain of the icy cave. Joey would gladly have changed his mount for Yarraman, but unless he rode Florian he had not the same control. In the saddle, controlling the bit, using the pressure of his knees, the touch of his hands and the sound of his voice, Joey was Florian's master. Astride another horse this would not be so.

On the seventh morning, after an hour's grazing, Brumby raised his head and trotted about, whistling to his mares. They surged together and Brumby drove them along the route he wanted them to go. It was time for Joey to control the herd and turn it in the direction *he* chose.

He whistled Reb and Bluey to him and cantered swiftly to where he meant to head off the herd. He heard the thunder of their hooves when he was out of sight down a piece of sloping ground. There was no snow, but the ground was hard and the wild horses' hooves made a ringing, hollow sound as they came towards him. He

turned Florian and rode to the top of the slope, then
shortening the reins he sent Florian swiftly across ahead
of the leading mares, shouting as he did so, and Reb and
Bluey shot ahead to turn the herd.

The leading mares swerved, then Joey saw Brumby
charging at him. Joey shouted, Reb was joined by Wolf
and while Bluey streaked ahead and kept the mares
wheeling, the other dogs combined with Joey's shouting
to turn Brumby after them.

So far so good. Joey slowed up and called his dogs
back to him while Wolf loped after Yarraman. Joey
worried that the horses might swerve again in their
original direction, but they did not. He looked down at
Bluey, panting, the saliva dripping from the frilled edge
of her red tongue, looking up with liquid eyes. He smiled
down at her saying, 'Good girl!' He was pleased with the
way Bluey worked, it was the first time he had asked
anything specialized of her.

He did not want to dismount Florian until he settled
down; the stallion was still taking dancing steps and
rippling his muscles. Bluey galloped round them de-
lightedly, pleased with the work she had done.

For two days things went well, with the horses going
in the direction Joey wanted them to. Then he stepped
up his interference, sometimes urging them on gently
when he thought they had fed long enough. By now Joey
thought they must be almost on the land which his
friends had mapped for him.

Then Brumby drove his mares at right angles to the
route Joey wanted them to follow. Everything had been
going so well that Joey was unprepared for this abrupt
move, and even with the dogs' help he could not turn the
herd once it was underway. So he followed patiently for
a couple of days until opportunity came and he wheeled
the mob in the direction he wanted them to go.

Florian and the packmare had both lost condition, but Joey was the thinnest of them all. His unrelieved diet of rabbit was revolting to him, his young face was gaunt, his long limbs and thin young body more coltish than ever.

Then one evening as he rode along with the herd drifting before him, the brumbies turned suddenly and began racing in the right direction. Curious to find what had started them off, Joey rode towards the clump of trees where they had turned. Down the bank ahead of him was a small fire, and near it squatted a half-caste Aboriginal boy. His horse was tethered near by; it shook its head and stamped, excited by the sound of hooves. The boy stood up and called,

' 'Lo Joey, so yer got yer 'erd!'

Joey stared for a second and then said joyfully,

'Dave! I didn't expect to see you, this is great.'

It was Dave, Mr Carroll's boy from Orooba, and it was a wonderful thing to happen to Joey who had not spoken to anyone for so long. He swung out of the saddle and shook hands.

'Yes, I found them – and that's Florian, I found him too. My word Dave, brumbies're hard to drive!'

'You bet, but you've got 'em goin' in the right direction.'

Joey frowned. 'I'm getting into fenced country, I don't know what to do about it but I suppose if Brumby can get through one way, he can get back the same way.'

'Come an' sit down, we'll 'ave a bit of tucker.'

'Not rabbit?' Joey asked anxiously. Dave laughed.

'No fear, real beef, the best. I got plenty. I got a bit'er feed over if your 'orses're short. My word, that Florian's a beaut, eh? Looks a bit thin on it though.'

Florian got his nose in the feed bag and the packmare had a small feed too. Joey sat on a log.

'What're you doing here, Dave?'

Dave stood up from putting sticks on the fire.

'The Boss sent me to find a couple of his pure-bred cows that were missin'. I found 'em all right, dead as mutton, don't know what done it. The Boss told me I was to keep an eye out for you, an' to tell you to bring your horses in at the end of the L paddock an' some o' us'll see you through with 'em.'

'That's like Mr Carroll. They're not too easy to drive, but give me time an' I'll get 'em through.'

'I'll draw you a map later, there's rickety old fence one end, the Boss says we'll rip it down and build a coupla wings to 'elp you get in.'

'That's the best news I've heard.'

'W'en the Boss like a bloke 'e'll do anythin' for 'im, an' 'e likes you, Joey,' Dave said simply.

'I wish I could do something for him,' Joey said earnestly and Dave grinned at him.

'You can, git them brumbies through an' th' Boss wins ten bob orf Thompson!'

Nothing had ever tasted so good to Joey as that steak. After they had eaten Dave took him a couple of hundred yards along the creek to where a broken, deserted hut stood. In front of it was a tangled hedge of blackberries.

'They ripen early down 'ere,' Dave told him as they picked and ate them until the purple juice ran down their chins.

Joey was up and away early the next morning. Dave gave him the last of the horse-feed and the steak, saying he'd be back at the homestead that night. Then with the end of a twig he drew Joey a map in the dirt.

'It'll take you three days ter git there, Joey, an' we'll 'ave the wings fixed by then. I take a short cut, but there're a coupla gates you'd never git that mob through. Your best bet is through Guthrie's land. Try an' miss 'is 'ome paddock, 'e's not like the Boss, nasty sort of bloke they say.'

'Right. You show me where it is on the map an' I'll try to steer clear of it.'

Joey studied the map, memorizing every detail. Then he said good-bye to Dave and rode off on the trail of his brumbies. Brumby had led his mob to drink at the creek, and when Joey rode near he whinnied and drove them up the bank again, eyeing Joey on Florian, tossing his mane and stepping high as he nipped any lazy rumps that did not get out of his way fast enough.

As long as Joey was on Florian's back the other stallion ignored him. But Florian was always excited when he saw Brumby, particularly when he was getting his mares together to drink, to graze or to move on. Whatever he wanted them to do, Brumby had his mares under control, he was a good master, keeping vigilant watch over his wives.

As Joey rode up from the creek where the mares had been drinking, he reined Florian in and looked around, taking in the country so as to pick out the way that would be easiest to travel from a wild horse's point of view.

Joey turned in his saddle to look all around, and behind him, on a small rise about half a mile away, he saw two men on horseback. Their horses were quite still, and the men sat with their hands folded on their pommels like statues, watching the herd move off. Joey did not quite know why, but the sight alarmed him. He hoped they were not two of the nasty Guthrie's men, the men Dave said were likely to object to his taking his herd across their paddocks. The men on the hill made no move and there was nothing Joey could do unless they did; he rode after the herd in his usual way.

The feed was good in the paddocks through which

they passed, and Joey saw no signs of any more horsemen or of the Guthrie homestead which he was trying to
avoid. The herd only went a short distance before they
showed signs of settling for the night. Joey was in no
hurry, he did not want to reach the corner of Mr Carroll's 'L' paddock before the fence had been taken down
and the brushwood 'wings' were built.

Florian and the packmare had another feed that night,
and Joey saw Yarraman in the distance, happily crop-
ping grass and guarded by Wolf.

'You silly old bloke, just to run with the girls you've
missed a good feed,' Joey told him from a distance. The
boy could hardly wait to eat his own steak; even a
couple of such meals made him feel stronger, strong
enough, he told himself, to tackle rabbit again if he had
to.

Next morning Joey took off his rabbit-skin coat and
rolled it in his valise. The days were warm, but at
evening he put it on again and kept it on all night. He
knew he was filthy dirty, but though the air was warmer
the streams were icy cold and he could not face bathing
in them.

Joey and the dogs camped as near the brumbies as
they could without disturbing them. Often in the night
some grazing mare would wake him by ripping up the
nearby stubbly grass. The packmare grazed among them,
and usually she ran ahead with the herd. At night, as
Joey lay warm in his rabbit-skin coat and blanket, with
the two dogs pressed against him, Yarraman came along
and nudged his shoulder. Joey put up his hand and
stroked the big horse's nose, talking to him softly. 'Having a good time, old feller? You help me to get the mob
home and I won't worry you.' Yarraman snorted once or
twice into the boy's hair and went on with his feeding.

Part Three

The next morning they were on the move early. They travelled along at a leisurely pace until after midday when a fence barred their way, and Brumby wheeled his mob at right angles to it.

They wandered along the fence and Joey followed; even Florian was sleepy and Joey not as alert as usual in spite of an apprehensive feeling he could not understand and tried his best to dismiss. He watched the multi-coloured moving rumps ahead of him, and decided that when they were home he must cull some of the mares before next season, and, if possible, replace them with fresh stock. His herd must not become inbred, that is the curse of all brumby herds and the reason why a good leader goes off from time to time and returns with new mares he has commandeered. Sometimes a bold stallion took mares he found beside sleeping stockmen, hustling his catch away to drive them back to become part of his herd, driven by the instinct of herd-survival and not merely by acquisitiveness. In this way Brumby had added at least a half-dozen mares to his harem in recent months; now he had forty-two mares all told.

It was almost mid-afternoon as the herd moved slowly down the side of the fence, plucking at the grass as they went with Brumby behind them, feeding too, and keeping a wary eye out for danger. Even he was lulled by the warmth of the afternoon and the wide empty spaces on his right, the fence protecting his left side.

The sound of danger came to Joey and the dogs as quickly as it did to Brumby. The still warmth of the afternoon was broken by the gun-shot crack of whips, the shouting of men. Brumby's reaction was instant. He plunged across behind his herd which at the first alarm had bunched together and broken into a gallop. The dogs had also been half-asleep, trotting lazily behind Florian with drooping tails and half-closed eyes, their tongues lolling from the corners of their mouths. They looked alertly up at Joey, waiting for the whistle of command.

Florian pranced a little and Joey looked over his shoulder. Over the top of the hill he counted seven horsemen. Brumby runners! For an instant Joey felt sick with apprehension. He took another instant to look more closely and thanked God that none of them carried guns; the coils of raw-hide hanging on their saddles and their cruel, long-lashed whips were bad enough. For a moment he thought of riding towards them instead of away, of trying to stop them. But even before he could consider this he knew it would be useless.

Subconsciously the boy remembered the two men he had seen sitting on their motionless horses on the rise the evening before, and he knew as well as if he had been told that these men had instigated the drive. If this was so then they knew that he was with the herd.

Suddenly he realized that the herd was away to a flying start and he decided that he would ride up to the men before they scattered on their galloping horses to try and stop the brumbies; perhaps he could delay them while Brumby got his herd away. He noticed the packmare and Yarraman were with the herd, only he and Florian and the dogs were left. He turned the big stallion and rode fast towards the men.

Inwardly Joey was heartsick. Even if he could save his mob, they would be scattered once more and he would have all the toil of getting a nervous herd together again. He shouted and waved to the men and in a few seconds he was close enough to see the grins on their faces.

None of them failed to notice the oiled smoothness of Florian's action, the beauty of his splendid body, but their mocking eyes saw also the queer little figure that rode him. It was just a boy with a thin, exhausted face and steady eyes, wearing filthy, ragged clothes, a rider, yes, but a boy, and it was good fun baiting boys; besides, that stallion looked pretty good.

'Let's see if we can talk him out of it!' said one of the men.

Joey reined Florian back. 'Good day,' he said politely, 'I thought I'd come back and tell you that the mob you saw are my horses, I'm taking them home.'

'Is that so?' the big heavy man with the crop of black whiskers round his blue-skinned jowl spoke with an obvious sneer and waited for an answer.

'Yes, that's so.' Joey spoke quietly and waited too.

'You mean they're branded? Wot's your brand?'

Joey looked steadily at him. 'No, they're not branded. They come from my Dad's place and they're our mob.'

The man swung one leg over the pommel and picked his teeth with the end of a small twig, drawling,

'Wot's yer dad's name?'

'Jim Meehan.'

'Never 'eard of 'im.'

'I don't suppose he's heard of you,' Joey said in the same quiet voice. The men laughed and the dark-faced one looked annoyed. One big lout added,

'I 'ave. I've 'eard of Jim Meehan, an' 'e can go yer, they tell me, Boss.'

Joey guessed that the dark man was Guthrie.

'Well, 'e ain't 'ere. That's not a bad moke you're ridin', boy, I think I'll try 'im out after them brumbies.'

The half-circle of men closed in a little. Joey's heart fell. Florian was the one horse he felt sure could overtake the brumbies, besides that, they were used to him, they would not be afraid when he approached them. Whatever happened he must not let them get Florian – yet what chance had he to stop them? They were seven to one. They had ropes and they would not hesitate to use them. Joey thought quickly.

'Wel-l,' he said doubtfully, looking round quickly to see that the dogs were beside him, 'I don't think . . .'

'Never mind wot you think, cum'orn, git down an' 'and that big brute over.' As he spoke Guthrie swung his leg lazily over the rump of his horse to dismount. That was Joey's cue. He kept Florian slightly on the move and now he shouted to his dogs,

'Sic 'em! Sic 'em, Reb!' and to Florian, 'Hup! Hup, boy!'

A chorus of surprised shouts, a grunt and a stream of curses came from Guthrie, who found himself instead of dismounting flung to the ground by his rearing horse in protest at its nipped fetlocks. Florian rose in the air from an almost standing start and sprang away. Joey crouched low in the saddle to lessen wind-resistance and whistled piercingly to his dogs.

Behind him all was chaos, rearing horses, and the furious Guthrie picking himself off the ground to remount his own horse, but Joey gained a considerable start. Florian flew like the wind and Joey let him have his head. He knew that by now the herd, knowing it was not being pursued, would have stopped or slowed up considerably, he also knew that his only chance was to reach them and to send them thundering on again.

Then he saw to the right of the trees what seemed to be a very old windmill. This was Dave's landmark on his dirt-map, the one he had chosen to indicate to Joey where the wings were to be built from the opened fence.

Joey's heart thudded with joy. They had a chance, his precious herd; not much of a chance though, he could hear the thud of the horses coming up behind him and he saw that Brumby, half-a-mile ahead of him, heard them too and he bustled his herd on. Joey looked back over his shoulder. Three of Guthrie's men were trying to ride up the fence so as to force the herd out into the open paddock where they could head them whichever way they liked. If they did this, the mob would never go through the brush wings Mr Carroll had built to lead them to the safety of his land. At all costs Joey must stop them.

The boy settled down in the saddle. He must not only overtake the brumbies before Guthrie's men got there, but he must ride up the side of the herd and head them into the wings at the right moment. He was calm now and he would not think of failure. He rode Florian as he had never ridden him before, mercilessly, but with every trick he knew of lightness in the saddle and delicacy of hands, and Florian responded magnificently. Faster and faster they flew and reached the tail of the herd where Brumby nipped and neighed and forced the pace, but the wild stallion took little heed of the figure he knew so well riding beside his herd. Joey looked back, the men were gaining. He drove Florian on, leaving the mass of the herd behind, and farther back again Brumby fought for their freedom, guarding their rear.

The men gained. Whip-cracks and shouting reached the ears of the now frenzied mob, but they did not break or turn. That grand old-stager, Yarraman, galloped after Florian, and Wolf joined the other dogs in holding the thundering brumbies steady.

Riding low, Joey gained the lead-mares. He heard the shouts behind him grow more excited, but he did not turn in his saddle; he thought the increased noise was the last effort of the runners to scatter the herd, and he had no time to think of anything but getting the mob-leaders between the short brush wings he could see before him. Another burst of speed and they would be safe on Mr Carroll's land. If Joey had glanced back then he would have seen a fantastic sight.

Two of Guthrie's men, whips cracking, voices raised to the high, frightening sound that brumbies fear, rode towards Brumby at the rear of the herd. In an instant the great stallion reared and screamed. With ears flattened and blazing eyes he charged straight at the riders. Their frightened horses became unmanageable. One man saw the stallion's lean, vicious head drive at his leg, and screamed as the savage teeth met above the knee and he was pulled to the ground.

Three other men galloped up, getting between Brumby and his herd and shielding the fallen man. Rope nooses shot out from their practised hands, Brumby reared and again his high whistling cry of fury rang out. One huge raised hoof caught in the loop of a thrown rope but the wild beating of his forehooves threw it off. He turned, wheeling round, and saw the men between himself and his fast-disappearing herd, then with all the splendid gallantry of a wild leader he galloped out on to the plain, using himself as bait for these unpitying men that they might leave his mares alone.

Guthrie and another of his men swore as they rode at the tail of the mob and saw the galloping mares led by Florian and Yarraman pour through the brushwood wings and into Carroll's property.

The herd galloped on for a few hundred yards and plunged down the creek bank, then, at the top of the bank, Joey turned Florian and rode back towards the opening in the fence. He meant to pull the brushwood wings across the gap and he hoped he was not going to

The savage teeth met above the knee and he was pulled to
the ground

have any more trouble with Guthrie and his men. He concentrated on what he was doing without glancing at a clump of trees to one side of the gap, or he might have seen Mr Carroll and his men waiting for him from where they had hidden themselves so that the sight of them would not make the herd swerve.

Joey's eyes caught sight of something else. Far across the paddock, brown-gold under the sun, he saw three horsemen struggling with their mounts, and at the same time trying to hold to a great white stallion they had roped firmly between them. Brumby reared and was pulled down by the ropes, the butt of a whip came down brutally on the side of his head and Joey cried out in pain and fury and rode forward. Then he remembered that what the men really wanted was Florian. He must not put another capture into their hands. In his misery he looked away from the brutal scene a mile across the plain, and he saw Mr Carroll and his men coming forward to meet him.

'Well done, boy!' he heard, but he shook his head dumbly, and pointed across the paddock.

'They've got Brumby.'

The men looked where Joey pointed, and swore. From the left came the sound of hooves and Guthrie and one of his men rode up. Mr Carroll looked at them with silent distaste. Dave walked over and stood by Joey's stirrup, and Joey looked down and smiled at the boy's upturned face that was full of distress for him. Both of them looked straight at Mr Carroll to get a clue as to their behaviour from him. Guthrie spoke first.

'Evenin', Carroll. We was runnin' some 'orses – brumbies, no brands – w'en this 'ere boy run 'em inter your land. The rest o' my blokes'll be 'ere soon as they 'obble that wild stallion we got, then we'll go in 'ere an' git the mob.'

'No you won't,' Mr Carroll told them quietly, 'I won't have any brumby-runnin' over my land, I've got some of my best stock in this paddock.'

'You built them wings on to *my* land.'

'An' we're takin' them down now. Thompson, George,' he turned to his men, 'Get goin' on the wings.' He turned back to the scowling Guthrie. 'Guthrie, this boy went off with his dog and followed those brumbies right up into the mountains more'n three weeks ago. He brought 'em back on his tod, an' as far as I'm concerned he's goin' ter keep them – besides, 'e's won me ten bob!' he turned his head and grinned at Thompson.

'That's right, Boss,' Thompson agreed.

Guthrie looked ugly. 'Well, we got th' best of th' mob, that stallion's worth a few bob.'

Joey broke in, 'Mr Guthrie, my Dad'll buy Brumby from you at a better price than you'll get from anyone else.'

Guthrie interrupted, glaring at Joey angrily,

'You young whipper-snapper, you won't git that 'orse agin, I'll see to that – unless you wanter swap th' one you're ridin' fer 'im?'

'There wouldn't be much sense in that,' Joey told him wearily. Mr Carroll broke in,

'You always 'ad a mean streak, Guthrie, an' you're showin' it now. You don't want that stallion, but you won't let the kid 'ave 'im. Can't you be a man for once – anyway, I'll give yer fifty quid fer 'im right now, an' that's more'n you'll git fer a brumby from anyone else.'

Guthrie looked furious and said, 'Thanks, I'll keep th' stallion.'

Without another word he turned his horse and rode away, followed by his men. In a detached way Joey noticed that one side of his shirt was dirty and torn and he could guess at the bruises beneath it; at least Reb had won one round from the bully when he nipped his horse and made it throw him.

The men stood silent as the others rode away. Mr Carroll put his hand on Joey's knee. Florian, having had all the exercise his big frame needed for the moment, looked as dozy as an old milk pony. Mr Carroll said,

'I'm sorry about that, Joey, but there's nothing else I can do. Brumby's unbranded, Guthrie's men have him. But I'll promise you this, if he comes into open sale I'll try to get him. But, knowing Guthrie, I think he's more likely to break him in and work him round the place, draggin' carts, that sort of thing.' He stopped abruptly at Joey's tortured face as he said,

'No, oh no! Not Brumby.'

The thought of that wild, powerful creature dragging a cart was not to be borne. But inwardly the boy knew that it had to be borne. He heard Thompson say,

'Th' son of a . . . 'e's mean enough to do that.'

Joey climbed wearily from the saddle, and he gave Mr Carroll a sad little smile.

'Thank you sir, thank you very much for what you tried to do.' He put his hand up forlornly and tugged at Florian's forelock. 'You know, he wanted Florian, they were seven to one and they'd 'a' taken him too, only I'd taught him a trick. So I set the dogs on Guthrie's horse and he fell and I said 'hup' to Florian and got away. I suppose they're pretty mad missing Florian.'

'Try and forget it, boy, your horses'll be safe on my place. When they settle down we'll get them together and put them into the paddock beyond the homestead. You'd better come in for a feed, you look like a sheep-dog at shearing. Never was much fat on yer, but there's none now. My word, the little bitch looks well.'

Joey looked down at Bluey with Dave squatting beside her pulling her ears.

'Yes, she's a good dog after the horses too. I'll help the boys build up the fence, Mr Carroll, I don't know what I'd've done without those wings.'

'I thought you might need it,' Mr Carroll said dryly, 'but the boys'll fix it in a few minutes. We've got the billy on. You remember old Charlie Li? Well he's made a bit er fancy stuff for yer, 'e says it's 'velly good' and I expect it is. Dave says you got stuck inter the steak all right. Well, you'll 'ave a good feed tonight, dunno 'ow you stuck rabbit all that time.'

'It was that or nothin'. Anyway, I couldn't've reached the mountains if you hadn't sent me along to Bruce Merry's. There was a blizzard and we spent a couple of days there an' Bruce taught me a lot about camping in the cold – he gave me two books too,' Joey added proudly, 'but I won't read them till I get home.'

'I knew Bruce'd look after yer. Now, come on, boys, a pannikin of tea's just w'ot Joey wants ter set 'im up.'

Suddenly Joey realized he was very tired indeed, his legs trembled as he walked, but if his mind had not been going every inch of the way with Brumby, he would have been very happy indeed. As it was the sorrow he felt over his horse sapped every other feeling, but he tried not to show how he felt. Mr Carroll and the boys had done so much for him it seemed churlish to let them see how troubled he was, so he forced himself to be cheerful.

The sun was dropping fast as they mounted their horses and Joey rode ahead to start the herd along the way without panic. It was not easy to get the mob moving as he wanted; they missed Brumby, but in the end they reached the outer paddock from the homestead, and with the help of the dogs and the Orooba men they drove them through a wide, slip-railed gap, and stood watching while the mares scattered in a rather bewildered way. Brumby had kept his mob on such a tight rein for years that they were lost without him.

'Now,' Joey thought sadly to himself, 'Brumby has given more than his life for his mares, he's given his liberty – oh, how could anyone take freedom from him?' He kept his thoughts to himself, but the men knew that the drawn look on his young face, the tired droop of his shoulders, was not so much physical weariness as it was sorrow for his silver friend.

It was like coming home to Joey to go back to the homestead. He walked straight to the kitchen to thank Charlie Li for the tucker he had sent him, and to get meat for his dogs. Wolf, probably remembering the fine food he had had before, turned up on temporary leave from Yarraman, and he was fed too. He lifted his shaggy wolf-head from his bone as he tore the last shreds of meat from it and walked over to rub against Joey's knees. Joey bent down and fondled his gaunt head. 'You're telling me you're sorry about Brumby, eh, old boy?' Wolf licked his hand, turned and loped off to rejoin Yarraman.

Joey looked with pleasure round the clean, bare little bedroom he had had on his first visit. Remembering all the nights he had spent on the frozen ground, he eyed the narrow bed with relish. Reb put his paws on the edge of the bed and looked inquiringly at Joey, and Bluey, who copied everything Reb did, put her two floppy paws up too and cast imploring glances at her master with her soft dark eyes. Joey smiled and shook his head.

'Hey! You've had your dinner, aren't I to have any? Get down, you dopes, it's not bed-time yet!'

The dogs took their paws disapprovingly away and Joey picked up his towel and soap – real soap – and went off to shower. The water was cold but wonderful and he stayed there, soaping himself again and again, removing the dirt of weeks.

The extra socks Rowena had given him were clean, he had a fresh shirt and decided to throw the filthy one away, but Charlie Li, hearing the shower going, came trotting along, picked up Joey's clothes and took them off to launder. 'It's good to be here, best of anything to have these sorts of friends,' Joey decided, rubbing his cold pink body with the rough towel. Now he was hungry. What a marvellous night it would have been if only Brumby . . .

The boy walked back to his room and combed his dripping hair. It was long and wild. 'Have to get Rowena on to that as soon as I get home,' he told himself, adding, 'one thing, they'll have the fencing done by now.'

He stood for a minute on the edge of the veranda before he walked along to find Mr Carroll. He heard Florian's impatient whinny; Florian was expressing disapproval at being kept in the stable by himself. Joey sighed; there was no Brumby to fear now, perhaps he should have left him with the mob, but that would make him harder to catch in the morning, so Joey shrugged his shoulders and went to find Mr Carroll. While they waited for dinner he told him about his search, and about finding Florian in what would have become his icy tomb.

'So if you'd done nothing more than that it would have been worth it to you, boy.'

'Yes, it would, sir. I'm sorry if I'm showing what I feel about Brumby, I know it couldn't be helped and if it hadn't been for you an' the boys I'd've lost the whole herd – and maybe Florian too.'

'I understand, Joey.'

'I know you do. You see Yarraman's father used to be boss of the mob. A brumby runner shot him down when

I was only a kid and I saw it. Brumby was a youngster then, sired by a fine silver horse, a stranger to everyone, we don't know even now where he came from or who he belonged to. He fought old Yarraman and turned him out of the mob and ran with the herd for a while, then he just disappeared and Yarraman took over again. All that silvery strain is the stranger's. He must've been a thoroughbred the way he and his stock look, and Brumby was the first foal born sired by him. When I was a kid I used to watch him by the hour from the hide-out I had overlooking the brumbies' stamping-ground. Then when he was caught and put in a buckjumping show he nearly killed a couple of riders and escaped. My Dad bought him for me from the proprietor of the show because I was sure he'd come back to us, and he did.

'So you see Brumby seems even more mine than Florian does. We never tried to catch him and brand him, I couldn't stand to see it, now I suppose it'd've been better if I had stood it.' He sighed and Mr Carroll stood up.

'Come on, son, nothin's like a good feed to make you feel better. Brumby isn't gone yet. If Guthrie sells 'im I'll git someone to buy 'im fer me, an' then 'e'll be your horse again.'

Joey stood up and looked earnestly at his host.

'Mr Carroll,'' he said simply, 'I thought the only people in the world like you were my Dad an' Geoff an' Bill, so maybe that's something I've really learned. You know there isn't anything you could ask that I wouldn't try to do for you, don't you?'

The old bushman patted the boy's shoulder. 'I know it, Joey. Just you keep on being the way you are; it does a man good to see real courage and determination, and by God, you've got plenty of both.'

Joey almost dozed off at the end of the splendid dinner

that Charlie Li brought in, and Mr Carroll sent him off to bed although it was barely eight o'clock.

'Thanks,' Joey stood up and manfully suppressed a yawn. 'I'd better get going early tomorrow.'

Mr Carroll nodded, 'I'll send Dave and Thompson along with you on your way. Those mares'll scatter without Brumby, you're goin' to 'ave a job with 'em.'

Hours later Joey woke to a deep-throated barking in the distance but, muzzy with sleep, he turned over and prepared to doze off again. Reb's anxious whining was joined by Bluey's.

'Oh, go to sleep, can't you?' Joey muttered, but Reb jumped to the floor and stood up pounding at his shoulder with his front paws. A shrill, high, whistling neigh came from the stables and Joey sat up.

'What's the matter with everybody?' he said crossly. Then he registered that the barking had been Wolf's – something was the matter with Yarraman and the herd.

Joey pulled on his clothes and went so quickly on to the veranda that he almost bumped into Mr Carroll, who had pulled on his riding trousers over his pyjamas.

'What's all the noise?' he asked. 'It's not three in the morning.'

'Something's happened to the herd. That's Wolf's bark, he never makes a noise for nothing – and Florian – Listen?'

The shrill, impatient neighing was accompanied by a restless stamping and kicking against the wooden half-door of the loosebox.

'Come on, my mare's in the other stable, we'd better ride into the paddock and have a look.'

Mr Carroll lit the stable lantern; outside the sliver of a moon gave a thin, shadowy light through which objects looked large and shapeless, but inside it was very dark.

They saddled both horses quickly and were just riding off when Dave appeared, his dark face invisible except for his shining eyes and teeth.

'What's up, Boss? We heard the noise in the quarters.'

'Probably nothing, Dave; we're goin' ter take a look.'

Dave stood scratching his head doubtfully as the two horses moved away into the darkness. He shrugged and turned back slowly towards the men's quarters. Just as he was about to throw himself down on his bunk he heard the sound of returning hooves coming at a fast gallop. He jumped up and called,

'Wake up, Thompson – Fred – hey, Clarry, wake up, the Boss's goin' ter want yer.'

It was a matter of seconds before the men were in their riding clothes and moving towards the stables.

'What is it, Boss?' Thompson asked and the others waited. Mr Carroll got heavily out of his saddle without answering, then he said,

'Come inter the house boys, an' I'll tell you.'

Joey and the men followed him into the living room without speaking, and he lit the lights. The men looked at Joey and they guessed what it was.

'Boss, 'as that stinkin' Guthrie 'ad the nerve to come on our property and run off them brumbies?'

Mr Carroll nodded, he could scarcely speak he was so angry, and he could not bear to look at Joey's tragic face.

'Yes,' he said finally, 'they've done that, the filthy lotta dingoes. The question is, are we goin' ter let them git away with it?'

'Too right we're not!'

'Then what can we do? Drag up chairs and git round the table an' we'll see what we can dope out.'

So the brown, hard-faced men got round the table and Thompson asked thoughtfully,

'D'you think they'll guess we'll be fly right away?'

Carroll shook his head. 'No, I think they'll give us till daylight to find out, that's about two hours. We saw one o' them disappear over the ridge but I wouldn't let Joey go then. It wouldn't 'a' done any good, only put 'em wise.'

'W'ich way do you reckon they were headin'?'

'It's my guess they're makin' fer Wattle Creek. The ground's too hard about there to leave any tracks, then if they went up the creek, not down towards Guthrie's, they'd git to Sugarloaf Hill, git around that and inter their own land at Danger's Corner an' out onter the stock-route. They know we can't touch 'em there so they can take their own time ter git back to Guthrie's. Maybe they won't bother to take the mares back, I expect they hoped to git Florian, now outer spite they might take the mares an' leave 'em to scatter along the stock-route now they've no leader.'

'I think you got it doped out pretty good, Boss,' Clarry put in. 'If a man's quick enough 'e could 'ead them orf at Egon's Jump?'

'Yeah, I thought of that. I s'pose there'll be seven o' them, we're only five.'

'Boss, a man's gotta 'ave nerve to ride down Egon's Jump, but if 'e did 'ave it 'e could 'ide himself with a good long rope an' 'e could 'ave that mean yeller mob orf their 'orses quicker'n you can say "Guthrie's a rat".'

'That's the idea, Boss. I reckon we've got th' nerve – I know Joey 'as.' Joey reddened as Thompson went on, 'Let's give it a go, we can't let 'im do that ter Joey, an' we're not bad with th' ropes, so 'ow about it?'

'Right, it's a go. Let's git goin'.'

The men trooped out. Mr Carroll went to pull an old coat over his pyjama-top, calling to Joey,

'Come an' put on one of these coats, son, it gits mighty

cold around dawn, an' we may 'ave to lay quiet for a bit.'

Joey was shivering already with excitement and worry. He felt better now there was something they could try to do. Reb and Bluey stayed close at his heels, knowing something was wrong. As they stepped out together Mr Carroll said,

'Joey, this isn't a matter of speed. We'll make the first ten miles fast, then it's a bad ride, across scree and down steep-faced rocks. It's the sort of ride you need a station nag for, one that knows the country, and we've got those. I'd like you to ride one er mine. Wait ...' he stopped Joey speaking, 'Florian's all steamed-up about the mob, what we need is silence, and he could wreck the whole plan. Leave 'im 'ere, old Fred'll stay, 'e and Charlie'll see to 'im, an' you take one er my 'orses.'

Joey thought a minute, then he said, 'Thanks Boss, I will.'

Dave brought in the little mob of riding horses from the home paddock. Joey picked out a sturdy mare and saddled her. In a matter of minutes they were off, sweeping out of the home-paddock gate and at right-angles to the way Guthrie and his men had started off with the brumbies. They rode fast; sometimes Mr Carroll led and sometimes Thompson. It was impossible to see the ground and the men let the horses have their heads. When they had been riding about an hour they were up in hilly country, rocky hills covered with loose stuff that rolled away from the hooves, but which the men assured Joey was not noisy enough to be heard by Guthrie and his men who were some miles away.

They rode in single file. There were slopes so steep that the sure-footed hill-horses simply thrust out their front hooves to break their descent with their hind legs. It was both an uncomfortable and a dangerous ride, but it was the only way they could go to have a chance of getting to the rocky ridge of Egon's Jump in time to be above the narrow defile through which the brumbies would be driven out on to the stock-route.

Joey felt a bitterness towards the mean men who did not want his herd, but who wanted to destroy it because he, with the help of the Orooba men, had foiled them the first time. But then he thought of the men like Mr Carroll and his stockmen, of Bruce Merry, so that instead of seeing the outside world distorted into an abode of brutal men, he realized gratefully the amount of true help and comradeship that he had found on his journey.

Mr Carroll, who was in the lead, reined in his horse and the others gathered around him as he said,

'You men know Hell's Slide, as one of you christened it, but Joey doesn't. Come here beside me, boy, it's too dark for you to see from where you are. Here, look.'

Joey moved his horse beside Mr Carroll's and looked where he pointed. His eyes were used to the darkness now, and he could see what looked like the static gleam of rough water before him, falling like a tongue between the two platforms of land, on one of which their horses stood.

'What is it, Boss? I've never seen anything like it.'

'They call that loose stuff "scree". Touch it and it starts runnin', an' you'll be buried under tons of it 'way down there.' He pointed to where the broad, dull strip disappeared downwards.

'Then how do we get across?'

'We jump it,' Mr Carroll said grimly. 'It's only about ten feet where it narrows between these rocks. The trouble is the awkward take-off and the landing. It's the only way, but boy, lift your horse up and over, don't touch it or you won't have a chance. We'll take it one at a time.'

'What about my dogs?' Joey asked anxiously.

'Hmm, I'd forgotten Reb and Bluey.'

'I could carry Bluey, she's used to the front of my saddle.'

'All right. Dave, hand Bluey up to Joey.'

Dave dismounted and picked up Bluey, who immediately went floppy and boneless. He deposited her like a soft velvet bundle in front of Joey. The placid mare made no objections and Bluey relaxed perfectly; she had faith in Joey. Joey looked down at Reb,

'Mr Carroll, I'll tell Reb to "sit" until I get over, then I'll call him. I'm sure he can jump it, but . . .'

'Never mind the "buts", Thompson's the finest man with a rope you ever saw, 'e'll be ready to git 'im if 'e jumps short.'

Dave rode up beside Joey. 'I rode the mare you're on over this, Joey, she can make it.'

'Thanks Dave, I'll bet she can – even if I can't ride 'er like you do,' Joey paid respectful tribute to the superb horsemanship which the half-caste boy shared with most of his race.

'You'll do, Joey.' In the half light Joey could see the gleam of Dave's big white teeth. 'I never seen the man I believe could ride Florian like you can.'

Joey felt really pleased. Mr Carroll said,

'I'll go first, then Dave, then you follow, Joey, and Thompson and Clarry last, and watch out, boys. Last time I was here I saw a kangaroo-rat chased by a fox jump into the middle of the scree. Even its few pounds of weight started that stuff runnin', but it bounded across so quick that it got away an' good luck to it. Move back boys, give me room.'

He backed his horse, making it dance a little against the bit so that it would not make its short run from a standing start, and then he drove the horse forward, leaped the gap and moved away from the other side. It was Dave's turn and he rode lightly as a bird, down in the saddle, to rise with the horse in a beautiful curve and land safely.

This was a new experience for Joey. He told Reb to 'sit', and then crouched low over Bluey and got the feel of the mare's mouth. He took her across the scree in a beautiful clean jump that got a 'well done!' from Mr Carroll. Thompson followed and Clarry waited until Joey, with Thompson beside him, rope in hand, called Reb,

'Come on! Come on boy, hup!'

With a rush and a clean bound Reb was over and Joey breathed again. Clarry's horse slipped as the sturdy, red-headed man took off. She sprang wildly and for a moment it looked as if she would land in the scree. Joey gave an anguished glance at Thompson, noticing the rope in his hands. Clarry's horse's front hooves made the bank, but his hind legs hit the scree. Like some newly-aroused great snake it began flowing, gleaming dully in the semi-darkness. The rope shot from Thompson's hand and instantly he wound the end round a cleat on his saddle and his horse pulled back against it. Slowly the struggling horse and Clarry arrived on the bank, saved from a suffocating death at the bottom of the well-named Hell's Slide. The only words Clarry said were a casual, 'Thanks, Bill.'

The journey from Hell's Slide to Egon's Jump wound downhill over rough ground with detours round stumps and jagged rocks. On the skyline the rocks loomed against a slightly paler sky where a few stars gleamed among a torn wrack of clouds. The silence was broken only by the grunts and snorts of the horses, the creaking of leather and the sharp jingling of bits.

'How long to daylight, d'you reckon, Thompson?' Mr

Carroll turned in his saddle to ask. Thompson considered a moment then answered,

'Less than 'alf-an-'our before she lights up a bit, Boss.'

'Good, that'll just about do us. We wanter git settled before the lead horses git below us.'

Joey rode along torn by worry about his horses and his thoughts of Brumby. He was also worried how five men were to tackle seven of Guthrie's men. The Orooba men all carried ropes, the Boss and Thompson had extra ones coiled about their shoulders and they carried stockwhips with sixteen-foot lashes and short, pliant handles. Joey had admired the Boss's stockwhip when it hung coiled from a peg in the hallway. It was a modern whip, beautifully plaited, with a pliant plaited handle. The old-fashioned whips had stiff handles of covered wood which had injured many a man in a fall after stock.

It was still dark when the horses slid the last ten feet down hill and Joey found himself on a kind of battlemented ledge. For about twenty feet a rocky wall of two feet in height fronted them, formed of broken jagged peaks of rock. Behind this was space for a dozen men to hide themselves from anyone passing through the defile below. A gleam of light showed on the eastern horizon, first herald of the sun. Joey asked,

'What about the horses?'

'Jump down, boy, Dave'll lead the horses up the hill and along to the right a bit where they'll be out of sight. Keep those dogs of yours quiet.'

'They'll be quiet. I'll give you a hand, Dave.'

Tripping and stumbling the boys led the horses out of sight and tied them to sturdy trees. As they walked back Joey asked,

'Why is it called "Egon's Leap"?'

'Aw, because a bloke named Egon useter bushrange around 'ere, an' one time w'en the police thought they 'ad 'im 'e jumped 'is 'orse across that gap on to the cliff there.'

Joey whistled, 'Phew! That was some jump!'

'Yairs, it was long ago, they say men were a lot better in them days.'

Joey grinned, 'They'd need to be, an' so would the horses!'

They found the men settled with Thompson in the middle. The Boss called Dave and Joey beside him.

'Git your ropes ready, boys, you're goin' ter need 'em. Now listen, the brumbies'll come first, gettin' up speed when the walls close in. Then, ridin' like the gentlemen they're not'll come Guthrie an' 'is boys. I'm reservin' Guthrie fer meself. Thompson'll git the man next to 'im, an' 'e an' I'll fix up the next two men. You boys an' Clarry gotta get the other three. I only hope they ride in a pretty close bunch. Rope 'em round about the elbers, an' if they come off their horses a bit 'eavy, don't let it worry you. Understand? I 'ope it won't be seven to five, but it might be an' then the quickness of the 'ands'll 'ave to deceive the eyes of those blokes.'

In the east the sky was bright and the air about the waiting men grew clear and light before they heard the sound of hooves, the grunts and small whistling neighs that herald the coming of a band of horses.

Reb and Bluey sat up looking alert, and Joey spoke softly but severely and they subsided. Each man crouched behind a sturdy piece of rock round which he could whip his rope. Joey peered to the right where he could see the track as it wound out of the defile.

The leading mares came in, moving quickly and snorting to each other as they hurried along, suspicious of the rocky walls. Right beneath him Joey saw Yarraman's broad shaggy back and Wolf's smaller shagginess beside him. Moonlight was among a knot of mares. Jocy looked affectionately at his friends. He knew that Yarraman would try hard to control the herd, but he knew too that he could not do it. He was invaluable in his place within the herd, like a sensible matron among a pack of giggling schoolgirls, but none of the wild mares would accept domination from any horse except a stallion.

The last mare passed through the defile and now the men could hear the lesser noise of the horsemen approaching. Each watcher eased himself into the most comfortable position, and Joey waited with a thumping heart.

Guthrie led, the dawn-light showing up his ugly blue jowls. Beside him, just a little behind, was Mason, his head stockman. In a little knot that would take expert roping, rode the final three men — so it would not be five against seven after all. The men rode with their heads down; they resented working at night to satisfy the boss's spite. Joey calculated that the spacing was just about perfect. By the time the Boss and Thompson had thrown their ropes, the three drowsy riders would be opposite Clarry, Dave and himself. He tingled with excitement, and the hands that held the long rope so delicately poised were wet.

On they came, silent, the only sound from the movements of the horses. Joey fixed his eyes on his victim, but he took a quick glance at the Boss and Thompson to reassure himself. They looked as solid and controlled as the rocks about them.

Then, in absolute silence except for the hiss of the raw-hide as it moved through the air, the Boss made his throw. Like a thin dark snake dropping from the sky it settled over Guthrie's heavy shoulders, slid down and pinned his arms to his side.

The startled yell he gave combined with the swish from the other lassos. The quick hitch round the chosen spike of rock was the matter of an instant before the

The startled yell he gave combined with the swish from
the other lassos

frightened leaps of the horses and the steady tightening of nooses pulled the men from the saddles.

Dave and Joey had thrown simultaneously and neatly, but in the excitement of hitching his rope for the steady pull Joey bumped lightly against Clarry and diverted his aim. The noose fell to the ground and amid the yells of the other men, the excitement of the plunging horses, the man who should have been Clarry's victim wheeled his horse to plunge back the way he had come.

The horse gathered itself to gallop, and no one saw Thompson flick out his long stockwhip with his left hand so that it wrapped itself with deadly sinuousness round the rider's neck. His fall was a heavy one as the horse galloped from beneath him. Thompson gave a smile of grim pleasure, the man was too winded to pull the lash from about his throat.

Meanwhile the Boss, with an even grimmer air, hauled on his rope until the bruised, surprised Guthrie, unable to do more than kick and yell, found himself hanging with dangling feet against the face of the cliff, helpless, beside himself with fury. The same treatment was meted out to the other man and two dangling forms hung there, the ropes cutting into their flesh, their faces full of rage and fear.

'Play 'im Joey, 'e's the biggest fish you'll ever catch!' Dave muttered as the boys kept their ropes at a tautness that kept the men from being able to get their arms free. When they attempted to get away, the boys exerted just enough pressure to keep them trussed-up. Then the Boss said,

'Hold them, boys. Thompson, you and Clarry come with me.'

They scrambled down the rocks and Joey and Dave followed them, grinning and playing their catches. The air rang with curses and shouts of rage.

'Go on, Bill,' the Boss said to Thompson, who trussed up his stockwhip capture and pushed him against the rocks. The Boss stood with folded arms, his whip coiled on his shoulder, his eyes on the two men swinging like giant cocoons against the cliff. Then he turned and gave Dave and Joey a hand with trussing their men, pushing them in sitting positions against the side. The Boss glanced at his watch.

'Not bad,' he said in a tone of satisfaction. 'Five minutes since the first of those robbers came into the defile and they're thrown and tied and their horses makin' fer the scrub!' He lifted the whip from his shoulder and sent the lash as gently as a caress against his victims' dangling, elastic-sided boots, to silence their din.

'Shut up!' he roared, losing patience. 'Shut up if yer want ter get down from there.'

'I'll git yer fer this, Carroll. I'll git th' law on yer, you ...'

'I said "shut up"! You listen to me, you pack er scum. First I'm goin' ter tell yer wot I think of yer, then yer can start fer 'ome; the ten-mile walk'll do yer good.' He stopped and turned to Dave. 'Dave, git one of our 'orses and round up their mokes. I'd like ter put their 'orses with your brumbies, Joey, but then this skunk could 'ave the law on yer. Dave, take off the saddles and bridles, and stick 'em out on the stock-route w'ere this lot wanted to put Joey's mob. Stack their gear agin the gate and come back 'ere fer the start of the marathon – lotta plug-uglies,' he finished disgustedly.

'Now,' he turned to the others, 'you blokes come back up the rocks agen and we'll let these little fellows down. You lot,' he eyed them coldly, 'if you got nothin' better to do than pinch a mob er brumbies from a kid that's given weeks er blood and sweat ter bringing 'em this far, then yer can think about it on yer walk 'ome. I never seen a sicker lotta bullies in me life, a lotta stinkin' bullies, that's all you are, an' I orta put me w'ip round the lot of yer.'

Ignoring Guthrie's lessening shouts of rage and threats for the future, they went back to the ledge and began to let down the ropes. Thompson leaned over and shouted.

'If one of yer tries to make a break until th' Boss tells yer to go, I'll bring 'im back on th' end of me w'ip.'

Guthrie and his men had taken considerable falls, the ropes cut into their flesh and they were in thoroughly bad shape, but none of the Orooba men felt sorry for them; the Boss took a savage delight in the thought that, when the story got around, Guthrie would never live it down. He betted Thompson that the place would be for sale within six months.

'Good thing too,' he said with satisfaction, ''e's never done a thing fer the district, an' we don't want blokes like 'im an' 'is jackals anyw'ere near our place.'

Guthrie came down with a bump. He tore furiously at the rope around his arms and looked with red, angry little eyes as his men were freed. There was not much fight left in any of them. If there had been Thompson, leaning over the cliff, idly holding his long, deadly whip, showed them how useless it would be to try to fight. Dave rode up, jumped off his mare and called cheerfully to his Boss,

'Guthrie's 'orses're all out on the stock-route, Boss, their saddles and gear're agin the rails, except I thought you might like this, just to remember these blokes by.' The Boss looked contemptuously at the whip Dave held out.

'Give it to 'em, Dave, I wouldn't give it 'ouse-room.'

Guthrie's bloodshot eyes fell on Joey, a mean look crossed his angry face. He spoke in a sarcastic voice.

'You, boy, you know wot I'm goin' ter do with that brumby stallion I got?'

Joey's heart sank. He had never considered that even a mean man such as this would do anything to Brumby out of spite. There was no doubting the menace in Guthrie's voice as he waited for an answer. Joey looked at him quietly and waited.

'I'm goin' ter shoot 'im just as soon as I git there to do it.'

Joey forced himself not to show what those words had done to him. The Boss spat in the dust.

'Only a skunk like you'd think of a thing like that, Guthrie.'

Thompson's and the other men's faces were furious. Joey forced himself to answer quietly,

'What good'll that do you? Brumby's a good sire, he might improve that weedy stock of yours.'

With all his heart Mr Carroll applauded Joey's courage in the face of what he knew must be a crippling blow for him. He knew, as Joey did, that the only hope for Brumby lay in convincing Guthrie that whatever he did would not matter to him. So Joey gave him a long, hard, contemptuous look and turned away, walking back towards Dave. Guthrie lost his head.

'You can larf at my stock, but I'll git that darned 'orse. I'll shoot 'im, I tell yer!'

'So you said,' the Boss replied coldly, 'and now you'd better git started; you've got a long walk, Guthrie, you and the rest o' yer scum, so git goin'.'

Because there was nothing else he could do, Guthrie humped his ugly shoulders, turned round and began walking. His men went hurriedly after him, while the Orooba men stood and watched their departing backs. At the end of the defile Guthrie turned and shook his fist angrily. His men trudged sullenly after him as he moved forward.

The Boss looked at Joey, but he said nothing. He knew the boy must be near breaking-point, with the taste of victory turned to ashes in his mouth. He felt the best thing was to round up the herd, let Joey see he had all the horses he loved together again, with one exception.

When Dave and Joey went to get the horses the boy found Wolf beside him. He had appeared in his silent, shadowy way. Joey felt it was because he wanted to show him that although Yarraman was his friend and must be cared for by Wolf, Joey was his friend and his master too, but Joey had Reb, and Bluey too, and so . . . Joey smiled down at him and told him to get back to Yarraman because they were all going home after all.

The excitement was over. Everything seemed rather flat until they came out from among rocks and trees and saw the brumbies scattered about the big paddock, and Joey's heart was filled with gratitude for his friends. Joey whistled Reb and Bluey away, and the men spread out. The dogs got the stragglers together, but the herd was woefully lost without Brumby, and because they were uncertain the tamest among them behaved in an indecisive way. Even with five men and the dogs they were difficult to drive and broke away continually.

'We'll put them in the far paddock, Joey, in case Guthrie's mob get any more bright ideas. They'll be on your route there. You git a good night's sleep an' we'll see you on your way tomorrer, eh boys?'

'Yeah, and watch out fer that Florian; 'e'll be pretty lively after a spell an' plenty good food.'

'I'll send the dogs to get the packmare out. They'd better get Yarraman too. I'll ride 'im, don't you agree, Boss? Then Florian can boss the herd. He'll soon lick them into shape, they won't let Yarraman lead them.' He looked worried and added, 'Yarraman does keep the inner block steady, he's a help when I'm drovin' them on my own, but I think the mares need a leader and that'll have to be Florian.'

'Let 'em both run with the mob, boy. Take the mare you're ridin' an' welcome; she's yours an' I'm glad fer you to 'ave 'er; she's not a bad old mare.'

'Oh, I couldn't do that, Mr Carroll.'

'Don't talk silly, boy, she's yours. I'll ...' He had been going to say that he'd send a couple of his men with Joey, but something stopped him. He respected the pride in the boy; to offer that kind of help would detract from the achievement of bringing his herd home himself.

'A nice kid,' he said to Clarry as Joey rode out on the wing. Clarry replied,

'Yer can say that again Boss, 'e's a real man.'

Joey rode back to them. 'I'd like to take the mare, Mr Carroll, and thank you very much. Next year, when you come to see my Dad and me, you bring as many mares as you like an' we'll be proud to have Florian sire their foals.'

'Thanks Joey, we'll discuss that later. Right now, boy, you've to get this mob home, that's all that matters.'

But to Joey, right then, feeling as though his heart was bleeding to death within his body, all that mattered was Brumby. His Brumby was to die at the hands of a cruel brute.

Desperate for the safety of his herd that he did not know were being driven to sanctuary by Joey, Brumby had turned and galloped straight at his tormentors. The three stockmen spread their horses a little apart and waited, armed with their long-lashed, short-handled whips, as the snorting, neighing demon charged towards them. They were not very happy at facing him, they

could have turned their horses and bolted, but the en-
raged wild horse would certainly catch one of the horsemen and that man would have little chance of escaping
with his life.

Reluctantly, the men stood together, their whips ready
for Brumby, his hooves thundering, his big body like an
express train rushing down on the frightened horses and
men.

He drove straight at the man in the centre and the
cruel whips snaked about his head, removing a piece of
one flattened ear, but the stallion never flinched. He
screamed his rage, his big teeth bared. His powerful
shoulder hit one mare and only the fact that she was sent
sprawling saved her rider. He went up in the air and
crashed to the ground – a heavy fall, but it prevented
those great teeth from savaging him.

The other two men closed in with ropes and whips.
Brumby rose on his hind legs, towering before them, his
silver belly shining like the sun on a cloud, his huge
hooves beating the air as he prepared to pound the life
out of the fallen mare before it could scramble to its feet.
Normally the stallion would not touch a mare, but
now the hated rider was to him a part of the horse he
rode.

Before those pounding hooves could reach the fallen
mare the noose of a rope was round them and the huge
silver-white body crashed to the ground. The noose snapped in the fall and Brumby rolled right over and got to
his feet again. But before he could charge forward more
ropes bound him until, plunging and screaming, tearing
at the ropes with his teeth, fighting with every muscle of
his big body, he found himself bound and helpless, a
Gulliver ensnared by a web of Lilliputian ropes.

The fallen man rose to his feet and mounted the mare.
He added his rope to those already tying the horse and as

Brumby's head snaked towards him, eyes evil, ears flattened, his head suddenly more like the driving head of a python than that of a stallion, the stockman lifted his whip and brought the short handle down on the head with a crushing blow. Brumby squealed with rage and the blood ran down the side of his head. The frightful contortions of his raging body seemed as if they must tear apart the tangle of ropes, but the strong raw-hide, hitched about a tree-trunk, held, and fighting every inch of the way the wild stallion was dragged along between the men.

After a mile of this both men and horses were exhausted. They stopped beside a clump of shade trees that had been left in the cleared paddock. While Brumby still pulled and wrestled with his captors, one man dismounted and cut a short, strong, rounded stick. This was to make a device called a 'stick-bit', which, once it is in the horse's mouth, allows him just enough breath to walk, but not enough to gallop or to struggle.

To get it securely into the stallion's mouth took the combined efforts of the men. Only fear of Guthrie if they left the stallion made them persist; in the end it was done.

Poor Brumby, who had lived in wild freedom, had galloped for miles drinking the wind, who knew neither weakness nor restraint, was sorely stricken by this torture. His struggles left him gasping, the need for more air rasped in his throat and turned his great muscular power to water.

At the home stockyards he was left in the centre yard, built to withstand the strength of outlaws. Two of the men, Gill and Duff, wanted to leave the stick-bit in the stallion's mouth, but Alf Mason opposed them, not because he minded leaving Brumby in misery, but because he had worked longer for Guthrie.

'No fear, the Boss'll want to break this 'imself – an' I mean "break". 'Ere, give us a 'and.'

So the stick-bit was warily removed. The stallion gave a mighty gasp and the air rushed into his lungs; he pivoted on his hind legs and charged his tormentors. The three men had already sprinted for the fence. Brumby, unused to fences, plunged against the rails as his victims scrambled over the top and dropped to the earth on the far side. Brumby snorted, giving his whistling scream and beating a tattoo with his massive forelegs on the rails about him.

'I've 'ad that 'orse,' Tommy Gill remarked, and the others agreed with him.

Left to himself, Brumby's red rage cooled, but the indignity he had suffered, his hatred of the men who had dragged him here, overcame him every now and again. He whinnied his rage, pawing the dusty ground, sending clouds of the dull grey dirt over the shining silver of his shoulders in the way of a stallion prepared to attack a rival.

In his quieter moments he moved about the round yard with its eight-foot fence, pawing the lower rails, searching for some weakness that would let him break out. He could not attempt to jump the high rails in such a confined space.

As the hours passed Brumby felt the results of his titanic struggles. He was desperately thirsty, but all about him was dry dust. Whenever he moved, his big hooves sent up small clouds of dust, and when he trotted round the enclosure, stopping to paw the dry ground, shaking his wild head, blowing and whinnying, the dust rose in clouds to increase his thirst. The caked sweat dried on his body and made him a paler silver than before. Then hunger began.

Since there seemed nothing else to do, he began spells

of standing quietly; but when he heard the stockmen, headed by Guthrie, on their way back after their first defeat at the hands of the Orooba men, the wild horse became excited again and pounded about the enclosure, arousing more dust for the torture of his dry throat.

Guthrie, thoroughly out of humour after the defeat by Joey that had saved the brumby herd, turned grumpily when he heard Alf Mason telling him,

'That's the stallion. My word it wasn't 'alf a battle, never thought we'd git 'im in th' yard.'

'Yer put 'im in th' round yard?'

'Yairs.'

' 'E can stay there fer a coupla days. 'E'll tame down without water or feed, then p'raps I'll take a look at 'im. Now, you blokes, those so-and-so's aren't gittin' away with this. Even if that wasn't a mob of as fine a lot of brumbies as I've ever seen, I'd still git even with Carroll an' that kid. Come on inter the office an' I'll tell yer wot we're goin' ter do.'

The men followed Guthrie into his office. Brumby heard the movement of horses near by. He whickered at them, but there were no answering whinnies, and in the utmost exasperation he sent his trumpet-like scream tearing through his dry throat.

Guthrie looked across the dusty table with a scowl, then he put his stubby finger back on the dust and traced the way he meant to go, first to Orooba, then driving the herd through the defile by Egon's Leap.

'We'll take the stallion the boy rode an' the best mares an' stick the rest out on the stock-route.'

The men left the office with sullen faces, resenting the idea of driving the herd through the night to satisfy the boss's spite. A brumby run was one thing, but taking the kid's herd for spite, and losing a night's sleep doing it, was quite another. Still, Guthrie was the boss. Tommy

Gill and Ted Duff strolled by the round yard. Brumby neighed angrily.

'I'd like ter give the poor devil a bucket of water,' Tommy said. The other man laughed.

'The Boss'll 'ave yer ears if yer do.'

They strolled away, stepping over a little trickle of water that came down the hillside. It was not six inches wide, and there was not enough of it to do more than to soak progressively into the ground in an advancing, ribbon-like strip.

'Windmill tank's runnin' over,' Ted remarked.

'Yairs, an' runnin' towards the round yard. The brumby stallion might git a drop yet if the wind keeps up.'

'Good luck to 'im,' the other said sourly, thinking of the broken sleep they'd all get that night.

Brumby's big body craved water so much that hunger ceased to trouble him; now and again a wisp of wind would bring the faint scent of the trickling water in that loveliest of all smells, wet earth. Brumby's nose twitched, but his longing neigh scarcely sounded through his parched throat.

It was nearing midnight, and still the restless stallion moved about the yard. Then he stood very still, proud head raised. Men moved about, faint sounds and gleams of light came from the homestead windows. Then came the movement of horses, the clinking of bits and the creaking of leather. Soon the sound of hooves receded into the distance and Brumby lost his tenseness. The demons of thirst tormented him more than ever.

He circled the yard, pawing and sniffing. The ground dipped a couple of inches under the stout rails on one side. In the little hollow this made, the waste water from the overflow made the earth damp. The trickle of water seeped and spread and Brumby pawed furiously, maddened by the scent, but he could not reach the sweet dampness. Steadily the dark patch spread, and the continual pawing of hooves hardened on frozen earth broke the ground into dry clods. Brumby, used to digging his food from beneath crusts of snow, was effective at it. He pawed frantically, scattering the dry soil he dislodged.

Made desperate by his dusty throat, Brumby measured the distance from the softened ground of the pawed-out hollow to the lower rail. He lay on the ground, thrusting his great shoulder under the rail and trying to push his way beneath it. The wood creaked, but it held, dry splinters tore his smooth hide; it was no use. He shoved his way back into the yard, but his dreadful thirst sent him back to tearing at the earth, every dry fibre of his big body straining to get near enough to put his tongue against the blessed dampness.

Brumby would not give up. When he tired, his thirst drove him on again. The clods flew and were scattered half across the yard, a bottom of loose dust lined the hole, beyond it the trickling water seeped nearer. Again he lay down and rolled his big body as far as he could beneath the rail — and stuck. He could get neither forward nor back; the delicious dampness still eluded him. He pushed with hooves and body; an inch was gained — again. The dry, splintery wood scored his ribs cruelly but he still struggled.

Suddenly his big barrel-chest was through. On the rail above him was blood and curled bits of hide that had been gouged out. With a kick and a heave he was out and on to his sturdy legs. He stood with his hooves apart, panting and wheezing from the dust. Then he put his nose to the dampness and nibbled frantically at the mud. It was liquid he needed and the thirsty soil absorbed the water as soon as it touched it.

Brumby lifted his head. Before him was another fence,

but this was a big yard with an ordinary two-rail fence. Without hesitating the stallion drew back against the fence of his newly left prison, then with a few swift strides he reached the other side of the big yard and sailed over the fence, beautiful as a silver seagull, marred only by the dark line of rapidly caking blood along his off-side.

Once over the fence, Brumby's nose followed the damp earth to its source near the windmill, where the big tank had overflowed. Ordinarily the strange, moving, clanking thing would have kept him away. In the hard, soaked ground was a pool of water and he sucked it dry. For a few seconds he stood in the utter bliss of thirst satisfied, his big chest heaving in and out, the asthmatic wheezing gone, enjoying not only the relief of his thirst, but the joy of pure air in his lungs.

He turned from the hilltop and looked across the bare country about him, lifted his splendid head and sent his wild, free call across the night. In their quarters the two men who had not gone with Guthrie stirred on their hard bunks and relapsed into sleep again.

Walking with exquisite precision Brumby descended the hill, turning his wild head from side to side. Before him stretched a wide dark land. Three of Guthrie's best brood-mares stood together in the gentle darkness of the starry night lit only by a sliver of a moon.

Brumby, trotting now, scented the mares and swerved towards them. Then with mane flying and eyes flashing, the great beast broke into a gallop, swept up behind the three mares and without more ado, nipping and squealing, he drove them before him. On towards the horizon, then into a creek bed where once again the stallion drank deep of the clear water.

On through a fence where the wires dragged between the panels, carefully lifting hooves, and the four passed through. Moving on through the night, covering the ground steadily, leaving many horizons behind them, they journeyed into the warm, spice-filled heart of the grey-green bush. Brumby was lord of a herd once more.

Part Four

After the brumbies had been put in the far paddock and the Orooba men reached the homestead, Joey was too restless to sleep as Mr Carroll suggested. He went out to the stable and joined Dave, looked after Florian, helped about the place and found the warm friendship of the men comforting to a heart sick with the thought of Brumby.

Wild thoughts of going to Guthrie's place and rescuing the stallion passed through his mind, but in his heart he knew that Mr Carroll was right. Guthrie, a greedy man, would recognize Brumby's value and perhaps sell him. But if anyone, especially a witness to Guthrie's humiliating experience, tried to take him, then Brumby would be shot.

Wearily Joey went about the work, trying by sheer tiredness to dull his conscious mind. In the afternoon he sat with Mr Carroll on the veranda and discussed the future of the herd. The old bushman, who had come up the hard way himself, had good advice to offer the boy on the breeding of his horses.

'You ought to get away for a bit, boy; go to an Agricultural College and study horse-care, their breedin' and their sicknesses too; you're bound to get trouble with wild horses kept from migrating. Fenced-in 'orses get softer than they would if they ran wild, an' you got to learn to combat that. Now, w'en I come ter see you this autumn, your Dad an' those other friends of yours, an' me'll git together and we'll talk it over. I might be able to 'elp yer a bit.'

Joey leaned forward earnestly. 'Mr Carroll, you've been a real friend to me. Neither my Dad nor I, or Rowena and Geoff an' Bill'll ever forget it. I think we'll all want to do something for you next time.'

The old man's face softened. 'I enjoy 'elping you, son. You remind me a bit of my boy; 'e loved this place. 'E wasn't much older'n you w'en a young horse kicked 'im on the head – and that was that. So you'll see that you and your Dad'll do me a favour if you'll let me do what I can for you.'

Joey was too moved to speak. Somehow his own sorrow over Brumby did not seem so important now.

That night, in spite of troubled dreams, Joey slept soundly and rose early to feed Florian, saddle his new mare and be ready to leave after breakfast. He found Dave already in the stable. It was not only that the two boys were much of an age that made them friends, they had the same interest in the land and in horse-breeding; Joey was more sorry to leave Dave than he was to leave anyone except Mr Carroll. Dave slipped the feed bag on the mare Joey was riding.

'Anytime you git that 'erd so's you want a man to 'elp you, Joey, remember me.'

'I will, Dave,' Joey said seriously. 'I'll ask Mr Carroll to bring you along with him when he comes, an' you can have a look around. It's not much of a place, but when we get a bit of money we'll make it pretty good for horse-breeding.'

'That mountain you was tellin' me about, an' all them rocks, oughta keep their 'ooves good, Joey?'

Joey nodded and lifted his saddle on to his mare.

'Yes, it does. I wish you could see them on a moon-light night. I always go up the mountain an' watch them gallopin' about on the river flats. You can pick out Brumby ...' He stopped and they went on with their work in silence.

Joey slipped a halter on Florian, who was full of good feed and energy after being cooped up for two days. He greeted Joey with a display of rearing, pretending to bring his hooves down on him. Joey called him an old fool and slipped under his chest, prodding his ribs, Florian squealed with delight, this was an old game, he danced about and nipped Joey. Joey looked into his bold, bright eyes and rubbed his ears. Florian bent his beautiful head and his rounded, whisker-decorated top lip protruded as he whickered appreciatively with gentle movements of his lips as Joey tickled his neck.

'This is your big day, boy,' Joey told him. 'Today you've got to take over forty-two mares and boss 'em, and don't tell me you won't like that!'

Florian pranced restlessly and Joey added, 'You keep that showing-off for the mares, you old fraud.'

He turned to duck out of the loosebox, hesitated and went back, putting both arms round the crested neck, so that Florian, conscious that the boy was unhappy, in that mysterious way that belongs to all animals who love one human being, lowered his splendid head and nuzzled Joey's face.

Joey pulled himself together and resolved to put Brumby out of his mind; he could not put him out of his heart, indeed he did not want to. He gave Florian a final pat and went out to where Reb waited for him and to Bluey, who sat with her soft eyes anxiously watching for him, her whole body expressing her love. Joey squatted on his heels and Reb sniffed at his ear in off-hand sympathy that said 'we men don't show our feelings', but Bluey adored sentiment and wallowed in it. She pushed her way on to Joey's knees, assuring him with every melting glance, every movement of her small pliant body that he was of supreme importance in her life, his happiness her only wish.

Joey fondled his dogs silently, then he rose and went in to breakfast. Afterwards he went to say good-bye to Charlie Li. He found him on the back steps, a bowl resting on his spotlessly aproned knees as he mixed a batch of johnny cakes for smoko. Above it his round, golden moon-face looked like a medal against the blue paint of the kitchen wall. Charlie Li looked at him sternly.

'You eat good bleckfus, Joey?'

Joey sat on the steps beside him and nodded.

'Full to bustin',' he replied elegantly. Charlie Li looked his approval.

'You bling saddlebags, we pack.' Charlie rose.

'But Charlie, I don't...'

'Bling bags,' Charlie said imperiously.

'I was only going to say that after all the good tucker you've given me, I can eat rabbit for a while.'

'No labbit.' Charlie waved the lordly hand that held the wooden spoon. 'Plenty good tucker, bling bags.'

That was a command. Joey grinned and went off to get his saddlebags. The packmare had been rested, and Mr Carroll told him to take all the dry feed he could carry. Joey was not worried about feed, the country would be fairly good and he did not intend to hurry the herd. In fact, with only himself and the dogs he could not hurry them.

He was delighted with the food with which Charlie plied him. He could have managed without it, but he would not dream of hurting Charlie Li by refusing it. He was touched by the thought and care Charlie gave to feeding him, and he said a regretful good-bye to the funny little figure in the white apron, balanced on bandy, blue-clad legs, whose whole effect was a roundness that matched his moon-face.

With the Boss rode Thompson, Clarry and Dave. Joey led the prancing Florian, who took a fancy to the stranger mare Joey was riding. Joey kept him in line by frequent slaps with the end of the halter, while he told him of all the ladies awaiting him within the next few miles.

The paddock in which the herd had been driven was only partially cleared. The leaderless herd scattered aimlessly. Joey whistled his dogs away and at his whistle Wolf came loping over the land, so he knew that Yarraman was close by. The dogs scattered and the men, waiting until the dogs got a nucleus of the herd together, sat sideways in their saddles, rolling cigarettes and talking quietly together.

Presently there was movement among the trees Florian whinnied and became more restless, rearing and curvetting about while Joey soothed him with 'Steady, boy.'

Three mares galloped out of the scrub with Yarraman at their heels, caught sight of the motionless horsemen and the restless Florian, who whinnied on the high whistling note that wild stallions use to their mares. The mares, manes flying and eyes wild, balked and wheeled, but two of the dogs anticipated them. They seemed about to scatter when Bluey joined the other two dogs, and Yarraman, whom in their freedom they despised, steadied them down. His large, comforting form made them hesitate; they turned their heads alertly, ready to break away, but drawn by the whistling calls of the stallion.

Joey slipped the halter off Florian. With the pride of his Arabian ancestors in every taut line of his shining body, Florian reared, whistled again and galloped towards the mares. Joey whistled his dogs back to him. The mares stood their ground until Florian was fifty yards away and then they scattered. With a burst of speed and a squeal of rage, Florian was after them. The bewildered Yarraman turned in a circle, and Florian reached the nearest mare, nipped her rump smartly and was off after another. In no time he had brought five mares together, using Yarraman, his old friend, as a centrepiece, and in case of any misunderstanding about who was boss, Florian gave Yarraman a quick nip as well. Thompson looked at Joey with a smile.

'There's no mistake about who's boss of that lot, eh, Joey?'

'Florian's boss all right, it's in his blood, after all, he's Brumby's son. I expect he'll get a bit above himself, and he won't take any notice of me, but I think he'll make for home and that's what matters.'

Joey whistled his dogs away again and the men rode out, working wide of the dogs. Florian gathered his mares and Yarraman into a tight bunch, trotting round them, head low on his arched neck, ears flattened, tail flowing and hooves lifted high at every step, the embodiment of threatening power.

Gradually the men and the dogs searched out all the strayed or hidden mares; as soon as they came within Florian's ken, he gave a threatening neigh to his already subdued herd, and met the newcomers with savage nips that brought them immediately into line. If any were reluctant to join his harem he nipped them harder, and the mares' hides, still rough and woolly from the snowy heights, had weals and sometimes blood streaks on their rumps.

One mare, determined to be difficult, refused to conform. Florian drew back a little way and sent his great hooves against her ribs. After this she meekly joined the others. Even his own mother, Moonlight, was not free of an admonishing nip. Joey, watching this, thought, as he so often did, of his first glimpse of Florian, a tiny smoky bundle of soft hair, still damp with birth, being nudged to his feet by Moonlight. He wondered if she recognized this great animal as her own son and decided that she did not. He hoped desperately that Moonlight was already in foal by Brumby. This year, he thought sadly, the spring foals would be the last of the Brumby blood his herd would know. He pushed the thought resolutely from him, and cantered off after a moving brown patch that lurked behind some fluffy young eucalypts.

When all the herd was gathered, Florian continued to circle excitedly around them, but he made no move to start them off in any particular direction. Joey said good-bye to Mr Carroll and his men with real regret. He could not express his thanks for all they had done, but they knew how he felt and they all shook hands and wished him luck. He turned to Mr Carroll.

'Boss, I can't ever thank you, but you'll bring those brood mares along to Dad and me, won't you?'

'I will, boy. Now, have a good trip.'

'Will you bring Dave – all the other boys you can spare too?'

'Someone's got to stay at Orooba, but I'll bring Dave anyhow.'

Joey looked worried. 'Mr Carroll, we haven't got a homestead like Orooba, only a bit of a shack, but Rowena'll put you up.'

Mr Carroll smiled. 'Don't worry, boy, we'll camp. Now, on your way, and good luck, safe journey, Joey.'

Joey whistled his dogs and cantered slowly towards where the excited Florian guarded his herd. They were all milling round with him by now, wild and excited, difficult to control. Joey thought of the wide, empty land through which he must drive them. He slowed his mare and the packmare down and whistled his dogs forward.

Presently, timing it so that Florian was on the side nearest him, the dogs sent the leading mares on the far side into a breakaway. They thrust out like the head from a coiling snake and went streaming across the land. He slowed his horses up. The herd appeared to unwind and instinct stopped Florian's circling round them. He pranced behind them until the uncoiling process was finished and the herd on the run in a stream of brown and silver backs ahead of him. Then he cantered sedately behind them. The leaders slowed a little, those behind quickened until the whole herd blended to start their long journey as a mob.

For a while Joey kept going, making sure that Florian was satisfied with the direction, then he dropped farther behind and turned to look back. Trees and hillocks, small gullies and roughnesses of the ground obstructed his view. He could not get one last look at his friends, so he turned his head resolutely away and followed the fleeing herd, keeping out of sight.

When Joey gave Florian the leadership of the mob he knew that the stallion would become wild, and have only one thought, the safety of his herd. After a day or so he knew too that he himself would be accepted by the mares again as a harmless follower as long as he did not try to get too close. This was satisfactory as long as the mob were not alarmed by any other rider, by some transport along an unmade bush road or by contact with another brumby herd. If the first two happened, then Joey and his dogs must keep them going in the direction of home. If the last took place then Florian would undoubtedly challenge the strange stallion, the winner to take both herds. This thought troubled Joey.

When wild stallions fought it was almost always to the death.

A certain amount of guidance was necessary to get the herd home because, even though vast stretches of land were fenceless, fences did occur here and there, and only careful mapping by his friends would help him to avoid them.

The first day went smoothly; only once Joey sent the dogs to turn the herd slightly. That night Florian moved up from behind the herd, where he normally travelled, and led the mares down a steep bank leading to a creek. From a spur of land farther down, Joey saw the horses wading into the water, bending their heads and sucking up the water noisily. They began to play, ducking their mouths in and out of the water, squealing and splashing as they pounded the surface with their hooves.

Florian drank his fill and retired to the bank, watching over them, turning his head into the wind, sniffing for danger. When the mares had their fill, Florian went back to the water, splashing his big shoulders with his pounding hooves and then walking up the bank again, watching his mares as they trailed up from the water and spread out to graze.

Joey made camp slowly. He missed the companionship of the last few days. He felt almost homesick as he took food from his saddlebag, good meat, a solid raisin-filled square of his favourite cake, evidences of Charlie Li's thoughtfulness.

The two dogs were tired, it had been a long day. Joey, as he always did, looked over their paws after they had their raw meat supper. The night was cold, and he enjoyed the comfort of Reb against his legs and Bluey against his back.

He looked forward to taking Bluey home, his father would like her. He thought about the fence and hoped that at home they would not be worrying because his trip was so much longer than he had thought it would be.

Joey woke in the first grey light of piccaninny dawn. He did not hurry. Walking to where he could overlook the herd he saw fuzzy dark shapes moving and knew that Florian was gathering his herd together to move on.

He had his breakfast, listening to the waking birds. The laughing, jeering call of a kookaburra made him smile. He had seen the parent kookaburras lining up their baby birds along a branch to give them lessons in laughing. They were to him the alarm clocks of his homeland and it would have been a sad morning if he had awakened without hearing them.

A faint mist hung over the land, and the sun, pale and cold, began to draw it up in ladders of light. The wavering blue smoke from Joey's fire looked solid against the misty background, and as the boiling water fizzed across the top of his billy he dropped in the tea and sniffed at the pleasant freshness, Charlie's damper was lavishly buttered and Joey enjoyed it and the hard-boiled egg he had with it. Then he rose and stretched, stamped out his fire and went for the horses. Their feed was saved for the evening, but having become used to morning feeds at Orooba they gave disappointed whickerings and Joey felt sorry for them.

That day they made about ten miles by Joey's reckoning. Next day, about noon, the herd took fright and went off at right angles. It took the rest of the day to get them back on the right trail again, and it was a weary boy, tired horses and dogs that camped that night with only a handful of miles gained in the homeward direction.

Joey stretched out on his blanket with a weary sigh, and Bluey promptly sprawled on his chest. He went to sleep hoping they would do better the next day, and slept soundly. Next morning, to his disgust he found the mob had turned again in the direction of its flight the day before, and once more he started off to bring them back. He looked carefully at his map, wondering if Florian was right and he was wrong. But after checking he was forced to believe that Florian, proud possessor of his first big herd, was not interested in taking them straight home. The continual riding after the herd, and the long process of turning them, was exhausting not only for himself but for his dogs and his horses as well.

Joey's journey home, on which he had started out with a high heart, became a nightmare. His horses became visibly thinner, his dogs were sore-footed and he hated having to whistle them off to head the herd back to him. He was so often over-tired himself that he could not sleep and his face became thinner than ever, his shoulders more angular; but he never wavered, the herd must be taken back to what was to become their permanent home.

After a few days the good tucker packed by Charlie Li was all gone. Joey, the horses and the dogs had now to forage for themselves.

A week after they left Orooba Joey decided that they were not much more than half-way home, forty miles or so. Aching with tiredness he climbed wearily off his mare where he decided to make camp. It was a sullen evening with echoes of thunder in the distance; a brief white light washed over him from far-off lightning. He went about the business of making camp. His packs were lighter now and he pulled them off the mare's back, rubbed her down and hobbled her loosely so that she could move about to graze. He unsaddled his other mare, murmuring, 'Poor old girl, you're pretty leg-weary.'

As he went about getting his meagre supper he decided to get Yarraman out of the herd as soon as it could be done without scattering the mares. Changing to a fresh horse, especially the strong, reliable Yarraman, would be a great help in following Florian's vagrant progress. Yarraman would be pretty wild now and he realized he must go after him before the mare he was riding became too weary. When Wolf understood that it was Joey who wanted Yarraman he would help to separate him from the knot of mares who were always around him.

Joey spread his groundsheet and put himself to bed. He was too tired to sleep and lay listening to the eerie cry of a bittern from its place by some pool. It boomed rhythmically, like the beating of a strange heart, and Joey yawned desperately, unable to sleep, his brain going over the legends Rowena used to tell him of how the Aboriginals took the cry of the bittern for the voice of their mythical creature, the bunyip. Descriptions of the bunyip varied with the tribes. To some it was a seal-like creature covered in long black hair; to others it was a frightening horror that lived on human flesh. Whatever it was Joey rather welcomed the noise it made. He counted the 'booms' for a time and fell asleep from exhaustion.

The tired boy slept deeply. Sounds coming through the night and the movement of the two dogs away from him made no difference, he was drugged by the sleep he needed so badly. Then something stirred in his hazy mind and he realized that all was not well. The night was dark. Every now and again, from the rolling storm-clouds that moved across the sky, lightning made silver selvages of their edges and muted flashes crossed the land. The air was transparent enough for dark objects such as trees and horses to make solid blacknesses in the midst of it.

Joey sat up, forcing back the sleep that drugged his brain. He pushed his feet out of his blanket and stood up. He heard low, warning growls from Reb, then the squeals of a horse and the thumping of heavy hooves.

He stumbled towards the sounds. A blur of white moved through the darkness, he heard the whistling neigh of a stallion, the squeals of a bitten mare and the clink of hobbles, the staccato tapping of the earth of the harried mare's front hooves as she tried to move away from the stallion's bites. Before Joey could call out, the hobbles broke, thunder surged across the sky, lightning flashed down showing him the silvery hind quarters of the big stallion. Florian was driving off the packmare.

Joey yelled, but the stealthy night foray of the wild creature that Florian had become made him ignore his former master. He had achieved the splendid isolation of a wild stallion to whom his herd is all, in whom nature's urgings found their primitive response. The herd must survive, to survive the stallion must find a plentiful supply of new blood. Florian acted according to his kind, the wild horse he had become through Joey's own action, and it would be useless to send the dogs after this wild beast that had taken a new mate.

The boy stood quite still in the dark shadows of the trees, lit by the nervous flashes of lightning, and he saw the mare, her hobbles broken apart, chivvied on by the stallion until they both galloped away, a dark moving shadow beside one that gleamed with the pale iridescence of the stormy darkness.

Joey turned away. He was too tired to think, too tired to realize what the loss of the packmare meant. There was nothing he could do until the morning, then he would think and plan; now he must sleep.

He lifted his weary head and whistled his dogs to him, pulling the blanket around him, sealing it at his back with the soft, burrowing form of Bluey, while at his legs lay the more solid Reb. He had a hazy feeling that he should worry, but he could only think of sleep. The bittern began its measured booming again, but this time Joey did not hear it, he was already asleep.

Daylight broke and Joey slept on. The sun was well above the horizon when he woke, having slept away the worst of his tiredness. He lay still for a few minutes with a puzzled frown on his thin face. He felt he should be worrying about something, but he could not remember what it was. Then he did remember. He sat bolt upright, and the dogs woke, injured at being moved so abruptly. Their long pink tongues came out in vast yawns, but Joey looked past them to where his pack-saddle leaned against the trunk of a tree.

He rose wearily to his feet, wondering if perhaps his other mare had gone too. He walked to the creek, hoping the cold water would wash the fuzziness from his brain. To his relief the mare was standing at the edge of the water. She had finished drinking and nodded her head up and down, watching her own reflection in the water.

Joey eyed her critically; she was not in very good shape. He rode light enough, but now she must carry his bedding too, he decided he must simply leave the old pack-saddle.

Joey had never considered the possibility of Florian taking *his* mares, and now he was in a nice pickle. If only Florian would make straight for home it would not be so bad, but this business of following the herd every day to bring them back to the right direction, with never a gain of more than a few miles, and only one mare to ride, was really serious. With himself, the dogs and the mare all so weary, he would not be able to cut Yarraman from the herd.

Breakfast was a sparse meal, the remains of a goanna

which was all he had found to eat the day before, and that was due to Reb, who had come into the camp, his jaws clamped on the throat of a seven-foot, grey and scaly beast with yellow stripes around its long tail.

Joey did not enjoy eating it, but he was hungry and it was all he had, so he ate part of his share and kept the rest for breakfast. It was not bad, cooked among the coals until the scales pulled off. The flavour was like rank chicken with a fishy taste through it. He hoped that the dogs would bring in even a despised rabbit through the day. Then he remembered how, borne down by weariness the night before, he had forced himself to make a small fish-trap between two boulders. He went to look at it half-heartedly, and found that it held two small fish. This cheered him, and giving the dogs all the remains of the goanna he ate the best part of the fish himself. Some of the weariness left him. He saddled the mare and started off.

For once the brumbies had wandered off in the right direction, and Joey rode behind them, keeping just out of sight. In the afternoon the horses veered northwards and he whistled the dogs off, and rode his tired mare along to turn them back. He saw his packmare meekly moving along near to Yarraman in the centre of the herd.

Joey toyed with the idea of trying to cut Yarraman from the herd, but he knew that if he excited the mob by getting too close, his leg-weary mare could not keep up, and the dogs were not enough for the whole job. No, it was better to plod on quietly, gaining a few miles day by day.

Next morning he found the herd had moved off in the night and were now heaven knew how many miles away. The boy set his teeth and rode after them.

Jim Meehan tamped down the earth around the last

post of the morning. He straightened his long back and stretched.

'Smoko!' he called to Bill Regan, who was delving away at a post-hole in hard rocky soil that would presently give way to earth that was easier digging. Bill slouched his way to Jim and together they boiled the billy and ate a couple of scones Rowena had packed for them.

Rowena and Geoff had taken the buggy and gone to Conway's Flat that day. Their store of food was running low from weeks of fencing during every moment of daylight, and at last they had to replenish it. They left early, with a list of their own and the other men's needs. 'It'd never do for Joey to get home and find us out of tucker,' Rowena said.

Now, with Joey more than two weeks overdue, they were worried; Rowena most of all. Jim said they would sink the last post-hole that day. The next would see the brush wings set up, and after that, with no more work to do, with the fence of Joey's dreaming a reality, they would really worry about the boy.

The last thing Jim wanted was to go looking for Joey as if he did not trust him to bring his herd back alone. Above anything, Jim valued his son's independence, and his trust in his father and his friends. They must be patient, but it was difficult.

For the hundredth time he and Bill sat on a log in the dappled shade of the river gums, and tried to think what could have delayed Joey for nearly three weeks beyond the time they believed it would take him to bring the mob home. Now Jim, his pannikin of hot tea in his hand, stirred it with a twig and made up his mind to say something to Bill Regan. He took a gulp of tea and turned to the other man,

'Bill, d'you think I ought to go after Joey?' Bill

considered the question, and Jim went on the defensive, adding, 'After all 'e's only fifteen, just a kid.'

Bill grunted. ' 'E may be "just a kid" but 'e's the best bushman I know.'

'Then you don't think I ought to go?'

Bill shook his head. 'No, I don't. I believe Joey's O.K. an' you oughta leave 'im to it.'

'That's all I want to know. I can't help worrying.'

'You take a look at Rowena,' Bill said dryly, 'I reckon she's lost pounds this last week, and she won't admit to worryin'.'

Jim laughed. 'She's game all right.'

'I reckon she thinks more o' the kid than if 'e was 'er own.'

'Me an' Joey's got a lot to thank Rowena for. With her to 'elp 'im Joey's got more ejercation already than I ever 'eard of, an' w'ile I wouldn't say so to 'im, I like to 'ear him talk nice the way she's taught 'im.'

As the horses trotted along the dirt road towards Conway's Flat, Rowena asked Geoff much the same question that Jim asked Bill, and she got much the same answer. They reached the little township and Geoff put Rowena down at the store. Then he fetched his horses water and tied them in the shade of a pepper-tree growing in the street. He followed Rowena into the store and bought his tobacco, then began ordering from Jim's list.

When the Bretts finished their shopping they walked down the street to where the one little pub stood, its broad veranda-roof shading the sidewalk beneath. In turn it was partially shaded by a row of tall pepper-trees with their small serrated leaves, their bunches of shocking-pink berries that smelled so horrid when you touched them.

Geoff went into the bar and Rowena ordered lunch for

them both. It was not a very elaborate lunch, cold corned beef and rather old carrots, but at least she had not cooked it herself, and she was determined to enjoy it.

There was only one large table. Overhead sticky fly-papers were festooned from the central light to the wall, and the stillness of the dining-room was disturbed by the buzzing of flies caught by wing or leg to the stickiness.

A burly bushman and his son of about twenty joined them for lunch. While they ate and talked, Geoff asked the men if by chance they had heard anything of young Joey Meehan and the mob of brumbies he was after?

'Funnily enough I have,' said Mr Young, and his son Andrew nodded and went on,

'Dad an' I ran into old George Carroll at Lagoons a coupla days ago. We were sittin' round after dinner an' George started talkin' about the kid. We thought he was pulling our legs, but you say the kid really did go up into the snow to find those brumbies?'

'He certainly did, but we 'aven't heard a thing, we don't know if he found them?'

'He found them all right, found his dad's stallion too I believe, then he started for home. Must have some guts, that kid.'

'He 'as,' Geoff said quietly. 'We're worryin' because 'e oughta've been back nearly three weeks ago.'

Rowena broke in, 'Oh, it's good to hear any news of him! I wish he'd get home, he must be worn out.'

'I tell you what, Andrew an' I're going north from here, we'll watch for the kid an' give him a hand if we can.'

'Will you? We'd all be so grateful. Tell him his fence'll be ready. He can't come too soon for me.'

'Mind you, it's a big, empty country he's goin' through, mostly "run rights" land, but if we see a mob of brumbies, we'll investigate.'

'I'm so glad we came to town and met you,' Rowena

turned her kind, plain face to the two men and thanked them again.

They drove home slowly because of the heavy load in the buggy. Rowena could hardly wait to tell Jim that they had news of Joey.

Joey, his nerves stretched taut by too little food and too much striving, lay trying to sleep. He had had quite a feed, but he hated getting it. He knew that he and the dogs must have some substantial food to be able to go on with this nightmare of a trip when, as fast as he took one step forward, he seemed to be forced two steps back.

He was deeply disappointed that the capricious Florian refused to make straight for home. The stallion kept the herd together and drove his mares in an exemplary manner, but he drove them in unpredictable directions. Trailing along in the rear, fighting to rectify matters, Joey, his only mare and his dogs, all suffered great weariness and despair.

Recognizing that much of their weakness came from lack of food, he forced himself to make a loop-trap from one of his raw-hide ropes. In it he caught a wallaby; it had to be killed and he did it as quickly as possible. He and the dogs ate well that night with something over for the next day.

He lay on his ground-sheet watching the half-moon rise and the cold light seep among the trees, turning the pale leaves to so many tiny pennants of misty silver. The sudden wild call of the stallion was borne on the night wind. Fainter, but unmistakable, came an answering brazen cry.

Joey's tiredness was forgotten in the realization that what he feared was about to happen. Florian was courting a fight with another stallion. How much would wild instinct enable him to hold his own if his opponent was the veteran of a hundred fights? Florian, his Florian could go down in the terrible destruction that a wild stallion can cause.

He did not know what to do. The wild stallion might run from a man on horseback, but, in the heat of battle, it would be more likely to savage the mare. He could not risk the poor thing which was already so leg-weary that it hurt Joey's soft heart every morning when he had to saddle her. On foot he could do nothing, yet he could not lie there and listen to those high, terrible neighing screams coming closer together. So he whistled his dogs to heel and walked up the rise dividing his camp from the wild horses so that he would not disturb them.

On the ground below him he saw a small hillock round which the mares grazed. On the hillock, splendid head high, mane rippling in the breeze as his wild call cut the night, stood Florian. Between each call the proud head went down and he snaked his crested neck menacingly, pounding the earth with his big hooves, throwing dust over chest and shoulders.

The mares had gathered uneasily on the far side beyond the hillock. A big, dark horse stepped from the trees. He paused and went through the challenging scream, the snaking and dust-throwing routines. Joey sized up the wild stallion; it was a big brute, powerful and aggressive, full of vitality, lacking the beauty of the other horse.

Joey rubbed his damp palms against his trouser-legs. His weariness was forgotten in an agony of fear for his own splendid horse. The wild horse drew nearer, Florian came off the knoll and lessened the distance between them. He pranced a little, his neck snaked, his ears flattened evilly against his proud head. Both stallions nickered and whistled shrilly, prancing and flexing their muscles. Joey waited.

They moved quickly together, rose high on their hind legs, front legs beating the air, teeth bared and heads twisting and darting at each other. Joey let his breath out as their forelegs came to the ground without either touching the other. Florian lifted his head with a screaming neigh and the two horses rushed together. From where he stood Joey heard the clicking of teeth that failed to meet flesh, then the silent seizing of hard shoulder-flesh, the release that left the rough dark shoulder and the smooth silver one with torn flesh glistening dark in the moonlight.

They wheeled, rose and pawed at each other, darting their heads, instinctively trying for the fatal grip on the jugular vein. They lunged together, their crushing weight smashing at each other, and then whirled away like giant cats, only to charge back again. Like a dancer Florian whirled, planted his front hooves firmly on the ground and his heels cracked like a whiplash against the other's ribs.

The wild stallion staggered, sprawled on its knees and Joey yelled at Florian to stop. Florian, knowing no more of fighting than instinct told him, saw his opponent slip and fall with a certain surprise, and then he heard Joey's yell and he flung his wild head round in the direction of the voice.

The wild horse, too, heard the yell. His brain, excited by fighting, remembered an escape from brumby runners and the yell that preceded the sensation of winged flame as a bullet ploughed its way through his fleshy rump. He scrambled to his feet, alarmed and unhurt, turned and fled from the voice of man whom he feared as he did not fear his own kind.

Joey gazed after the wild horses; he could not believe that the encounter was over. He watched Florian, still excited and victorious, trot proudly on to his knoll

They moved quickly together, rose high on their
hind legs

and send his high cry of victory across the moonlit world.

Knowing the wild stallion would not return, Joey went back to get some sleep. For a time he felt the earth shake beneath the high-stepping of Florian's hooves as he circled his herd, whistling and whickering, too excited to settle down.

By the next night Joey reckoned they must be about twenty-five miles from home. He looked at his own thin hands, what a scarecrow he was! His dogs too; gently he ran his bony hand over Reb's ribs; although Bluey was a fine dog after stock, it was Reb who was the leader, and he took the brunt of the work. Bluey was thin too; her hide was so loose on her body that to touch her felt like slipping a furred grape out its skin. Not much longer now, Joey told himself, surely they would make it now.

He rode slowly along in the heat of the morning, praying the wild horses would not make a rush in another direction. The blue sky was cloudless, and in the distance one range of hills lay behind another in a succession of blues known only to Australia. A line of darker trees probably edged water and he turned towards it; they all needed water.

Instead of shady, inviting banks, the little creek flowed through a thick crop of dry burrs. Joey took his mare through a narrow track made by stock and at the water's edge he dismounted and drank beside the mare, who stood with her front hooves in the water and sloshed it round her bit. They rode along the water's edge until the burry growth stopped. Before them a steep bank rose covered in dried mud, weeds and sticks, rubbish left by a flood of perhaps several years before.

The mare set about picking her way up the littered bank, slipping as dry clods of earth gave way, or making sticks crack beneath her hooves. They reached the top and went through a patch of hock-high grass. The mare gave a snort of fear and reared away from something Joey could not see through the dry grass. Joey looked down as he reined her in and saw a greenish-grey twist with a shadowy black pattern on it around her off-fetlock. The mare plunged with terror and the grey band uncoiled itself and slid swiftly into the denseness of the grass-roots.

Joey's heart sank. He recognized a tiger snake, the most venomous snake of all; it must have been barely missed by the mare's hoof and so had struck at her. If it had bitten her there was no chance of recovery. He rode to just beyond the high grass and leaped to the ground, picked up the hoof and tried to find fang-marks. He ran his hand firmly round the fetlock and looked at his palm. His heart sank, across it was a tiny smear of blood. He told himself it could have come from a scratch, a splinter from the dry sticks, but he did not believe it. He could not even find the spot to excise it and perhaps get rid of some of the venom.

Sometimes a dog, more often a dingo, recovers from snake-bite, but never from the bite of a tiger snake. The bitten dingo finds its way to the nearest water and lies submerged in it. Instinct tells the wild creature to do this, the coolness of the water slows down the circulation and the venom does not spread so quickly. The most usual bite was from a black snake which haunts the banks and is almost amphibious, and black snake venom is very different from the venom of the tiger.

Gently the boy led the mare down the bank and into the water. He pulled off the saddle and threw it on the bank. Her eyes were dazed and she swayed a little. Joey stayed quietly beside her, knee-deep in the water, rubbing her ears and talking to her out of his desolate heart. He did not love the mare as he loved Florian or

Moonlight or Brumby, but he was fond of her and he hated to see her suffer such a mean death.

Presently her legs gave way and she collapsed into the water and Joey held her head out of it. Gently he removed the bridle. The mare scarcely breathed; the venom collapsed her lungs; in half-an-hour it was all over.

Joey waded ashore. He looked at the useless bridle in his hands. Well, it wasn't much to carry. He pushed his saddle into the bole of a hollow tree. He was straightening up when he thought he heard voices. Glancing back at the still body of the mare, a brown mound in the shallow water, he climbed to the top of the bank with Reb and Bluey at his heels.

Riding along the crest of the bank were two men, a burly elderly man and a younger one. The young one glanced up and saw Joey, and called out, 'Good day.' The two men rode up to him, eyeing him closely, and Joey, exhausted by weeks of hardship and shattered by this latest blow, stood erect by a great effort and gave them back a grave, 'Good day.'

The two men saw a thin, exhausted-looking boy of fifteen with steady blue eyes set in a dirty brown face, his fair hair long and untidy, his clothes dilapidated, creek-water seeping from the cracks of his boots, a scarecrow of a boy who looked steadily back at them, until a smile crossed the older man's face and he said,

'Don't tell me, I know; you're Joey Meehan!'

'Yes, I am, but how did you know?'

'My name's Young, this is my son Andrew.' Andrew swung himself off his horse and held out his hand to Joey while his father went on, 'We seem to've met a lot of your friends lately. First it was George Carroll.'

Joey's face lit up. 'Oh, how was he?'

'He's fine. Then, over lunch at Conway's Flat we

talked to Geoff Brett of Euro Downs an' his wife – they asked us to keep a look-out for you.'

The tiredness in Joey's face faded a little. Mr Young dismounted and joined Joey and his son. Joey wanted to know if they'd heard how his Dad was – and Bill Regan?

'Steady on, boy! Your Dad's O.K.; they're all pretty impatient for you to get back, the fence is finished.'

Suddenly the light left Joey's face.

'What is it, boy?' the older man asked gently.

Joey turned towards the creek and pointed to the brown bulk in the water.

'That's the mare Mr Carroll gave me. A tiger snake got her nearly an hour ago, the water didn't help. Now I can't pull 'er out.'

The men looked at the dead mare, the wreck of all the boy's hopes, and he stood silently beside them. Almost as if he was talking to himself Mr Young said,

'So you're beaten, boy.'

Joey straightened his shoulders and said in a shocked voice,

'No fear! It can't be much more than twenty-five miles. I've my dogs and I'll do it on foot – it'll take longer, but plenty've brumbies've been herded on foot before this!'

Mr Young looked down at the boy and said quietly,

'Your friends're right, you're pretty much of a man, Joey Meehan.'

Joey's exhausted face flushed. 'I couldn't let my Dad down now, nor the others either, not after they built that fence for my mob.'

'Andrew,' Mr Young turned to his son, 'we'll move along the bank a bit after we've pulled that poor devil of a mare out of the water, an' we'll boil the billy and have some tucker, Joey, we've got plenty, an' we want to hear what you've been up to, and work out something a bit better for you than herdin' those brumbies on foot.'

Joey went to the hollow trunk where he had cached his saddle and brought his ropes back. The horses pulled the mare out of the water, then, without looking back, Joey walked away with his new friends.

They found a flat, shady stretch of bank, boiled the billy and Joey tucked into a good lunch and told them about his adventures. The dogs, too, got a feed, and then he walked down to the water and rinsed the billy. While he was away the Youngs had a quick word together. When he came back he found Andrew pulling the saddle off his horse. Joey had eyed the horse for some time. It was a fine animal and he admired it greatly. He looked up in surprise when Andrew turned to him and said,

'Joey, Dad and I want you to take my horse and get on your way.'

'Oh! I couldn't do that, what'll you do?'

'I'm takin' Dad's horse. He'll wait here. I'll be back this evening with a spare horse for him. The Wilsons're only about nine mile from here across the creek; they'll lend us a moke.'

Joey looked from one to the other uncertainly. Mr Young put his hand on the thin young shoulder. 'Don't refuse, Joey; we couldn't face George Carroll if we let you go after that lot on foot.'

'We'd both like to think we helped you, we'll feel it a lot if you won't let us do what we can.'

Joey made up his mind. 'My friends've helped me so much I don't feel I've done anything. If you really want to lend me your horse I'll be glad to take him. I'll do my best to look after him, an' I'll bring him back as soon as I can.'

'No fear! We'll come and get 'im, we want to take a look at that herd of yours.'

Joey beamed. 'Then Dad can thank you properly for

helping me. I wonder if people're as nice everywhere as they are in the bush?'

'What about Guthrie? He wasn't too nice!'

'Him!' Joey's nose wrinkled with distaste. 'He wasn't a bushman, he was just a rat!'

'Well, you'd better get goin', boy. I'll walk back with you, I expect you'd like to use your own saddle, and there's a bit of tucker left, do you for a day or two. Andrew'd better get off. I'm goin' to have a sleep under one of those big gums up there till he gets back.'

Joey saddled his new horse, said good-bye and rode off with his heart full of gratitude. The Youngs watched him go; he turned in his saddle and waved to them. Andrew said,

'By jingo, look at that skinny, half-starved kid and think of all he's gone through in the last few weeks, and if we hadn't come along he'd of been after that mob on foot!'

'He looks good on a horse. I'll bet you, Andrew, if he hadn't had help from people like George and Bruce Merry and us, he'd've got home just the same if it took him five years to do it!'

Andrew nodded. 'Well, I'm glad he didn't have to. Does a man good to see a kid like that.' He put his foot in the stirrup and mounted his father's horse. 'Go an' have a sleep, Dad. I'll be back before you know it,' and he rode away.

A meal, and the feel of a strong horse under him, did Joey as much good as a couple of days' rest would have done. The horse was a tough bush waler and Joey decided not to go after Yarraman and excite the herd. He would be home before long, unless the mob became excited and dashed off in the opposite direction. If they did that, Joey thought grimly, he had a fresh horse now and he would bring them back. He hated the thought of having to tell Mr Carroll what had happened to the mare.

After half an hour he picked up the herd; they had gone off from the straight line he wished on them, but not very far. Next morning he and his fresh horse would drive them into line. That night Joey slept soundly, and he was up and about by the time the brumbies began moving. To his delight, a homing instinct seemed at last to touch Florian, and that day they made a good ten miles in the right direction.

Almost a week went by since Geoff and Rowena came back from Conway's Flat with news of Joey. Each day dragged past. It comforted Jim a little that Rowena was even more anxious than he was himself. Where was Joey? Jim was usually to be found at the Bretts', where the subject of Joey was debated endlessly.

A log fire burned in the open fireplace in the Bretts' kitchen. On iron bars across it stood the big, sooty-black water boiler with the wood-burning stove next to it. The kettle began to steam. The Bretts and Jim and Bill sat around, their wooden-legged kitchen chairs tilted back to a more comfortable angle. Rowena was busy at the table; she looked up and said,

'Joey's going to be here soon, I can feel it.'

The others jeered at her, but she only smiled and went on with her cooking with a brief, 'You'll see.'

'Pretty good the kid findin' Florian,' Jim said, trying to keep the pride out of his voice.

'I didn't give 'im Buckley's chance,' Geoff admitted. Bill's rather grim face softened.

'Just like the little bloke,' he said.

Rowena said nothing. In a way she could not explain she suddenly felt that Joey was near. For weeks she had worried about him being outdoors on these cold nights, until she reached the stage when she did not care tuppence for anything Joey might have accomplished, or might have failed to do; all she wanted was the boy to come safely back among them.

'Well, maybe you're right, Rowena, it can't be long now,' Jim said, more to reassure himself than because he really believed it.

Another day dragged by, and still no sign of the herd or Joey. Rowena had to put up with a lot of chaff, but she held out, Joey was near, she knew it.

Jim unsaddled and fed his mare. After a cold shower he set off for the Bretts, a determined look on his lined face. He had made up his mind. He must know what had happened to Joey. When he reached Euro Downs he told the Bretts what he had in his mind and Rowena nodded.

'I'm glad you're going to look for him, Jim. I know he isn't far away, but he may need you.'

Geoff looked down at his pipe without speaking, then he made up his mind.

'Yes, I'm glad too, but what about Joey? You know what an independent little cuss he is. Unless he's in a real jam I reckon 'e'll want to finish the job himself.'

'What d'you think, Bill?'

'I think Geoff's right. But if I was you, Jim, I'd go just the same!'

'You two're a fat lot of help! Right oh, I'll make up me own mind. I'm off after Joey tomorrer.'

Jim spent a disturbed night. He was not quite sure that he was right in going to look for Joey. On the other hand he was deeply worried about the boy. So many accidents can happen to a man alone in the bush. All night the thought of these hazards chased each other across his mind, fire, a bad fall, snake-bite . . . he tossed and turned and was glad when pale fingers of light came through the small windows and he knew that it would soon be dawn. He pulled a sweater over his shirt, for the dawns were very cold, made tea and ate some damper. Then he packed a saddlebag with food, lifted his coiled ropes from the wall and went out to the stables.

Jim's mare, Brownie, blew a cloud of steam into the cold air, she disapproved of leaving her warm stables at this hour. Jim, his mind on Joey, took no notice of her sniffing and snorting, her curtsying at the long shadows of dawn. He rode away from the shack across frost-crackling brown earth, across the creek and the big red plain beyond, where the earth had cracked in places to form wide seams which had always worried Joey when he saw the young colts racing across them. Then on to where the wings were spread to turn the brumbies into their newly fenced area.

Jim jogged along, alert, watching for tell-tale hoof-prints, and from each little rise he scanned the distance, hoping against hope that somewhere beyond him he would see the living dots that meant the brumby herd was on the move homewards.

It was mid-morning when, with the dirt-track rising ahead of him and a steep bank to his left, Jim turned his mare and rode up the bank to where he knew he could look over a plain stretching to the skyline. With grunts and heaves Brownie pulled herself up the bank. At the top Jim reined her in and shaded his eyes against the oblique rays of the sun.

His heart leaped. Far across the yellow-brown of the plain he saw first the sunrays touching the pale silver hide of a big stallion – Brumby? Or Florian? He didn't know. His eyes moved beyond the herd, past the sudden glimpses he got of the stallion, and Joey was there. It must be Joey, though the rider on the brown horse was too far away to be seen clearly.

The man moved his horse among a cluster of half a dozen small eucalypts. Standing there he watched the herd take on the shape of horses in place of moving blurs, at last he could even see that it was Florian who trotted and wheeled in the rear of the mares. Where was Brumby?

Then he could really see Joey, riding a strange horse, but Joey, his boy, a ragged skinny youngster riding like a veteran. Presently he picked out Yarraman with Wolf trotting near to him, then Moonlight. Crossing in front of Joey's mount he saw Reb and another, a stranger-dog, the bluey-grey of the famous breed of 'heeler' cattle dogs.

So Joey had made it! At this rate he would be back a little after four o'clock, Jim calculated, then he made up his mind and rode his mare down the bank and on to the dirt track below. He set off for home at an easy canter, determined that Joey's friends should join in the home-coming as they would wish to do.

Jim rode round by Bill's selection, and Bill saddled up and rode back to Euro Downs with him. Rowena and Geoff were about to have their dinner and Rowena insisted on Bill eating with them, but Jim would not wait. Clutching a large beef sandwich to please Rowena, he rode off again.

Now that he was almost in sight of home, Joey's exhaustion fought with his triumph. He was very glad that after all the careful turning, the remote control which he and his dogs had exercised, Florian was actually heading for home himself. He began to chivvy his mares, and instead of the long hours of grazing in the past, interspersed with the desire to move on in any direction but the right one, now the splendid head sniffed the breezes, the intelligent eyes looked towards home, and the rump of any mare who tried to slow up was severely punished. Back and forth, back and forth, head weaving up and down, the stallion trotted behind the bewildered mares, who could not understand why they were not allowed to graze in their usual desultory fashion. It seemed that an intense excitement and a tremendous energy gripped the stallion as he drew near his home.

Yarraman and Moonlight too seemed to catch some of this excitement, and while the stallion guarded the rear they kept in the front ranks leading the mob steadily onwards, and Joey thought to himself, 'if only they'd travelled like this from the beginning we'd've been home weeks ago!' Reb and Bluey both had tender pads from continuous running on hard, stubbly surfaces. Joey looked down and spoke to them encouragingly.

Now they were level with the brumbies' own mountain, and from the top of the next rise Joey saw the long brush arm that would block the mares from swerving towards the river. He began to ride out wide on the right side, whistling his dogs to him.

Jim rode to the top of a rise from which he could watch Joey's approach, and he reined in his mare. His heart was filled with love of his son, and with a great pride in him too. Joey had done this, Joey and his dogs, they had brought all those horses home through country that was alien to him, a journey that would normally take half-a-dozen well-equipped men with an intimate knowledge of the land to accomplish. Jim's hard brown face had a softness on it that no one but Joey had ever seen touch it.

He saw his boy riding well out from the herd, catching up with the leaders. Behind the horses, Florian, his excitement reaching fever-pitch, neighed shrilly, plunged about nipping his mares and whistling excitedly as he drove them onwards.

The leading mares saw the long wing and balked, looking wildly around, while the ones behind drove them on. Joey called his dogs, and riding low he sent his horse just beyond the leaders and closed in with shrill cries of, 'Yip! Yip! Sic 'em, Reb, sic 'em, Bluey!'

Yarraman pushed to the front so that, driven by Florian in the rear, the mares turned in an arc and flooded through the opening in the fence. Once inside, they spread out across the red ground they knew so well, and thundered onwards towards their mountain corral, while Florian with tossing mane and streaming tail neighed and whistled them forward.

Jim rode towards his son. Joey watched until the last brumby went through the gap, unconscious of anything else. Then Jim saw him drop his head on his chest, saw his shoulders droop, saw the whole weary sag of the tired young body as he cantered towards him.

'Joey! Joey boy, you made it!'

Joey looked up and smiled crookedly at his father; his eyes were very bright in the shadows surrounding them, and his thin face was desperately strained. Jim brought his mare beside Joey's horse and put an arm round his son's shoulders. 'What is it, son?'

Joey said one word, 'Brumby', and Jim understood that at the very moment of his triumph Joey was telling him that something had happened to Brumby to tarnish his victory.

'Come on, son,' he said gently. 'The others're all waiting for you under the trees.'

Joey pulled himself together, and father and son rode through the gap. The Bretts and Bill were there, and he slid off his horse and threw the reins to Bill while he hugged Rowena and smiled a happy, tired smile at them all. Rowena said,

'I've taken supper for us over to the shack, Joey, I thought you'd like to have it at home tonight.'

Joey put his arm round her tall shoulders and thanked her. Then he said,

'Dad, Geoff, Bill, will you help me to get the rails up? I don't want to lose the mob.'

'We'll do it, Joey, you look all in, get along with Rowena.'

'Chocolate cake!' said Rowena. Joey said,

'Not yet, let me help here first. If we just pull the brush off the wing across here, it'll do, none of them'll leave the mountain tonight. I must get Florian and Moonlight. If I don't put Florian back in his own paddock I'll never do anything with him, you'd think he'd been a brumby all his life the way he goes on. With you all to help I can get him and Yarraman too, and shove them all in the other paddock.'

'He's got four mares waiting for him.'

'Good, that'll keep him quiet. The mob can do without a leader for a few days, maybe altogether now that the fence's finished.' He remembered suddenly and said, 'Thank you for the fence, it's a lovely job, the best present I've ever had.'

'Joey, if it'll do to pull the brush across now, we'll rail this bit tomorrow. Now you get along with your Dad and Bill and leave it to me. The sooner Florian's in his paddock the sooner you can git a rest. Rowena an' me'll fix this.'

'Thanks, Geoff. Don't do much; then you and Rowena come along to the shack and I'll have a *big* slice of that chocolate cake, whatever anyone else wants! Shall we get going?'

They mounted and rode off. There was not a brumby to be seen. As they rode quietly up to one side of the mountain to where they could look down on the corral, they saw Moonlight and Yarraman standing together, staring in the direction of their old stables, and Joey smiled.

'We needn't bother about them, they're as good as on their way home already!'

They watched the big, almost ugly horse and the elegant little mare step out of the corral and start down the mountain, and Wolf left them briefly to come over and be made a fuss of by his old friends. Joey looked down at him, then he dismounted and rubbed the big dog's ears saying,

'You old fraud, you weren't nearly as much use as Reb and Bluey – oh Dad, you haven't met Bluey, I'll tell you how I got her later.'

Florian's intense excitement had died down. He, too, knew that he had reached home, and he remembered his comfortable stable and regular feeding. He watched Moonlight and Yarraman go with a puzzled air, but he did not rush forward to stop them. Then he walked slowly to the home-side of the corral, proud head moving up and down in a puzzled way. This corral was an exciting goal to reach; it was not his home.

Joey, a halter over his shoulder, stepped out quietly and spoke to Florian, Florian started and shivered, flung his head up and down and eyed Joey. The boy moved closer. The great hooves stamped and Florian neighed. Joey came closer, Florian moved as though he would break away, changed his mind and stood listening to Joey speaking quietly to him. He came forward a step, stretched out his neck and Joey moved in, rubbing his ears, whispering to him. For a time the outlaw was dead; the Arabian, servant of man through the centuries, was born again.

Rowena's heart mourned over Joey's young-bird boniness, the tiredness in his face and in the shadows about the eyes that sometimes looked startlingly blue. The three men did not show it, but they, too, were shocked at the physical evidence of the hard times Joey had endured for nearly two months. No one mentioned Brumby, no questions were asked; in his own time Joey would tell them everything.

The men followed as Joey led Florian back to his old paddock where Moonlight and Yarraman already waited for him, and the four strange mares gathered at one side eyeing their future lord. Jim opened the gate and Joey led Florian inside and slipped the halter off.

Florian's head went up, he sighted the mares and something of the master revived in him, the possessive screaming whinny of the stallion rang out. With neck arched Florian trotted about busily, gathering the four mares into an even tighter bunch and driving them before him just to establish his supremacy. Joey smiled at his father.

'The old show-off!' he said fondly. They turned away and joined the others to walk back to the shack where Rowena had tea for them with Joey's favourite hot scones and honey, a chocolate cake with thick icing; treats he had loved since he was a little boy.

Joey went and showered, throwing out his tattered clothing, the boots that barely covered his feet, the remains of the thick wool socks that he told Rowena had saved his life. When he returned they saw more clearly than ever how painfully thin he had become, but on his tired face was a look of peace, and Rowena comforted herself with the thought that she would soon fatten him.

After tea they sat and talked until Rowena moved them from the table while she set it for dinner. Outside the moon was almost full; the cold winter daylight did not seem to die, it merged imperceptibly into the platinum-cold of the moonlight. The big luminous moon hung like a silver tray in the sky, and the black shadows it threw had much the same sharp edges that the sunlight gave them.

Joey told them his adventures; of the kindness of Mr Carroll and of Bruce Merry. That reminded him, he disappeared and went out to the stable. There he felt in the bottom of a saddlebag and pulled out the two paperbacked Westerns and brought them back. He smiled broadly as he showed them.

'Now I'm home I'm going to read these! Bruce gave them to me and I promised myself I wouldn't read them until I reached home. Now I really am home.'

He sat down and went on with his story; the finding of Florian; the discovery of the mob; the return of Guthrie's men, and of how Mr Carroll helped him outwit them, but could not help him to save Brumby. His voice faltered as he told them about Brumby, how he had turned back and charged the men to save his mob and had been captured. Then he went on to tell how Guthrie had sworn to shoot the imprisoned Brumby.

The men's faces were grim, and Joey looked up, as he had done so often as a child, for the comfort of Rowena's sympathetic eyes. The story went on to Florian's leadership of the mob, and that last awful moment when the tiger-snake destroyed the mare Mr Carroll had given him, and his decision to bring them back on foot.

'But Joey,' Jim said in a puzzled voice, 'you can't drive brumbies on foot.'

'Why not?' Joey turned to Rowena. 'You remember reading me stories about the mustangs in America, and how men used to trail them on foot and in the end they drove them into corrals? I remember about one man who thought he *was* a mustang, he'd been trailing them for so long, he must've gone a bit mad because he threw off his clothes and followed the herd for hundreds of miles! I'm glad that didn't happen to me! I reckon that mustangs're only brumbies somewhere else; if those men could do it then so could I, but I'm glad that, thanks to the Youngs, I didn't have to try.'

Geoff smiled at him. 'You didn't only bring the herd back, Joey, you made a lot of friends as well!'

'Mr Carroll and the Youngs're coming to see us, and they're bringing mares to Florian.'

'Son, I think I'm prouder of the kind of friends you've made, than I am of your bringin' home the 'erd. Your friends'll always be welcome 'ere, an' there's no question of stud fees.'

'I told them you'd feel like that. I know how much they helped, but you an' Rowena an' Geoff an' Bill mustn't forget that when I got the mob here it wouldn't 'ave been much use without the fence, they might've strayed off again tomorrow, or I might've had to go after them every year. I don't think I've told you how wonderful it is to find it finished, I really haven't thanked any of you properly.'

Long after the meal was cleared away they still sat on, talking, keeping up the fire. A dozen times Joey looked about him hardly able to believe that he was really home, so happy that he did not notice how tired he really was. These were 'his' people, their faces reflected their pride in him. They kept the talk away from Brumby, but asked Joey to go over the rest of the story time after time until Rowena said,

'I think Joey should have a good night's sleep, he must be very tired. We must go home, Geoff. Bill'd better bunk-down at the house tonight.' She paused, her head raised to listen, and added, 'Ssh! What was that?'

'That's a stallion screaming,' Joey said and rose to his feet. 'That darned Florian must've broken out of his paddock; I'd better go and bring him back.'

'Leave him till morning, son, he'll be O.K.'

'I think I ought to get him, Dad, he's the only one

likely to get over that patched-up gap we left in the fence, but if he does, the others'll follow. We'd better get on to those rails first thing in the morning.'

Again the high, challenging scream rang out, and the faces round the table looked puzzled. That cry came from Florian's paddock. Without a word they all rose and followed Joey out in the moonlight. Two stallions were challenging each other across the moonlit paddocks.

Joey walked swiftly with the others following, until he reached a vantage point where he could look across the wide stretch of fissured land that spread from the foot of the mountain to the bottom of the sloping hill on which the shack stood, and out beyond that to the limits of the new fence.

Again the fierce call rang out. It seemed to come from the direction of the tangled brushwood that had been pulled across the gap through which the brumby herd were driven. Joey's heart thumped with excitement, a hope he tried to suppress rose in him. He ran ahead of the others to where they could see clearly in the moonlight that something moved beyond the camouflaged break in the fence.

It was not a stallion's cry, but the squeals of bitten mares, then high whinnies of annoyance as, crashing through the brushwood, five horses streamed, dark blots in the white light, moving quickly over ground that had a thin glitter of frost across it. The five running horses spread out a little and from the other side of the trampled brushwood something silvery-white appeared. No one spoke, they all held their breaths, and, beside Joey, Reb and Bluey whined questioningly.

Beyond the brushwood, rising in an effortless curve, appeared a great silvery body. This horse did not stumble and crash through the twigs and boughs but rose like some great white bird above it. Joey knew.

Brumby the foal, nosed to his feet by his mother

'Brumby! My Brumby! He's come home, he's not...'

Joey's eyes stung and he turned away. The great phantom of a horse charged across the ground, neighing and whistling, keeping his small herd together. When he got them bunched to his liking he drove them before him, and the pale light glittered back from mane and tail and shining body. Across the fissures, scarcely halting in his stride as he straddled them, along the foot of his mountain, up the rocky way that led to his secret place.

Already Joey was heading down the hill and the others followed. They crossed the creek and climbed the hill to Joey's look-out, the place from which, even as a very small boy, he had spent a part of every day watching his loved wild horses. This was the place from which he had seen Brumby the foal brought down by his mother from the mountain top where he was born, coming down on his infant legs, slipping and sliding, nosed to his feet by his mother; a foal as smoky and beautiful as his son Florian had been years after.

A thousand memories flooded Joey's brain as they reached the look-out. Below them the new mares mingled with the old; almost fifty mares milled there; weaving in and out among them, whickering and bullying, Brumby re-established mastery.

'Thank goodness I took Florian away at once,' Joey said. 'I wonder how Brumby escaped – not that it matters; all that matters in the whole world is that he has come back.'

Brumby, from the centre of his herd, raised his battle-scarred and splendid head, and told every listening creature within miles that the master was home again.

Joey, no longer even tired, went back home with his father and his friends, his journey over, his life just beginning.

If you have enjoyed this book and would like
to know about others which we publish, why
not join the Puffin Club? You will receive the
club magazine, *Puffin Post*, four times a year
and a smart badge and membership book. You
will also be able to enter all the competitions.
Write for an application form to:

The Puffin Club Secretary
Penguin Books Limited
Bath Road,
Harmondsworth
Middlesex